Rear View Mirror

Rear View Mirror

ISBN
Printed in Canada, October 2009

Books available From:

Annette Gray
GRAYTWEST BOOKS
Box 835,
Markerville, Alberta
T0M 1M0

janegray@telus.net

Website: www.graytwestbooks.com

Rear View Mirror

Take A Journey Through Alberta's Exciting Past

Annette Gray

To chart our future we must understand our past.

(annette gray)

Table of Contents

Foreword

Albertans, like any other geographic group, are defined by what we have seen and where we have been. Who we are and what has happened in our lives, give us a sense of belonging and joins us with others who share our experiences.

Rear View Mirror is a series of short stories about individual people, natural and man-made landmarks as researched and told by Annette Gray.

Her background of English parents who homesteaded in a difficult farming area gives her a life setting shared by others. Her stories are the stories that will invoke remembrance in other Albertans and provide details that illustrate for readers what we share as Albertans.

Each story is a special part of our Alberta mosaic.

Janet Walter

Former President of CAHS
(Central Alberta Historical Society)

Stories found in the *Rear View Mirror* were originally published in *Central Alberta LIFE*. Requested by editor Cameron Kennedy, these history based columns appeared every other week, 2007 through 2009.

Acknowledgements

I wish to thank all those who played a part in compiling the stories written for the Rear View Mirror.

What a pleasure it has been to sit, visit and record some of the finest and most interesting stories Alberta has to offer.

Special thanks goes to LIFE editor, Cameron Kennedy, for his ongoing support; to Janet Walter and Murray Fuhrer for their kind words; to my devoted proofreaders, Evelyne Heringer and Elaine Rutschke, as well as my old friend and cover-designer, Dave White.

I'm particularly indebted to sister Doreen who not only suggested I publish this book, but helped make it happen. Thanks Dory!

Thanks also to the many folks who patiently sat through interviews or answered questions by phone. The wealth of information and encouragement you provided is very much appreciated.

Rear View Mirror is dedicate to my best friend and husband of 50 years, Dennis, the fellow with a zillion stories and one heck of a knack for telling them.

Annette Gray

Introduction

Historian David Crabtree once wrote succinctly, "History is important." I remember my grandfather and even my parents spending a great deal of time and effort teaching my siblings and me about our family history.

Grandfather believed that understanding our past would help us understand our place in the present. I suppose my parents believed that a solid understanding of the past would lead us to build solid foundations for the future. Both my parents volunteered on local history book committees. The stories they and fellow committee members captured and preserved helped to form a glorious historical tapestry for all to read and enjoy.

Times have changed—rapidly changed—and today many people seem to define themselves not by where they've come from but by where they're going. The focus is on the destination and not the journey. In doing so, many are missing the rich history unfolding around them.

I have had the great joy of knowing Annette Gray and her fine husband, Dennis, for many years. Annette is a wise and sensitive writer with a great talent for finding the story within the story. Never satisfied with just scratching the surface, Annette is a writer who must peel back every layer of the proverbial onion to find the sweet core within. I admire that quality greatly.

I wasn't surprised to learn that, like my parents,

Annette had chaired history-book committees. The stories Annette has crafted are rich and varied in colour and texture, touching on a time, yes, but more importantly, on the places, events, and people who lived them.

History *is* important. Don't be so foolish as to believe that we live in a time so different from the past that these stories will fail to shed a light on our own existence. All things bring us awareness—especially our shared human experience. We must have a good understanding of the past in order to know how to deal wisely with the present. These stories are priceless.

Murray Fuhrer

LIFE columnist (Extreme Esteem),
and founding member of
Red Deer & District Writers' Ink

Rearview Mirror

'Invisible people' thriving in the Markerville area

It was an extra hot day in July—warmer than the inside of an Icelandic volcano. Yet folks still came to sit in the shade and catch a bit of ancient Icelandic history at Historic Markerville Creamery.

That's the day a large rock behind the creamery was officially recognized as the new residence of the Huldufolk.

Who are the Huldafolk? Well, they're the "hidden people," the mythological folks who are said to have come to the Markerville area as early as 1888, when Icelanders settled along the Tindastoll Creek and Medicine River.

Mythological stories are very much a part of the Icelandic culture, and stories told about the invisible Huldafolk are said to date back to A. D. 874, when Ingolfur Arnarson, a chieftain from west Norway, set up housekeeping on the present-day site of Reykjavik, the capitol of Iceland, thereby establishing the settlement of Iceland.

You'll have to admit 2,881 years is a long time ago. Superstitions ran rampant back then, so stories of invisible people with supernatural abilities were easily believed and no doubt enhanced as each generation repeated the Norse mythology.

Although Markerville's Huldafolk are reported to

Keen eyes might spot six little people in the above photo. Warning—only believers are able to see them!

be harmless folk, many of their counterparts were cruel little scamps. During the thirteenth century, Icelandic children dreaded winter as they were told this was the season when evil trolls came to feast on naughty children. The legend caused Icelandic children so many traumas that legislation was passed making it a felony to perpetuate this myth. Soon after, less frightening stories emerged—stories of gentle, unseen spirits with human traits, similar to the Huldafolk who were welcomed with open arms in Markerville.

Wayne Linneberg, a member of the Stephan G. Stephansson Icelandic Society, was on hand at the recent event to give a detailed sketch of Markeville's Huldafolk. He says they resemble humans, can be big or small and live, die and give birth similar to the human species. Wayne also explained the origin of the Huldafolk to the audience, saying that when God paid a visit to Eve in the Garden Of Eden he asked to meet all of her children. However, Eve showed Him only those children whose faces were clean. Those with dirty faces she hid, thus the all-knowing Father declared the children with dirty faces should remain hidden forever.

Does this theory lead to the assumption Markerville's Huldafolk have dirty faces? Perhaps. At any rate, Linneberg, who admits to studying the comings and goings of Huldafolk for some time, also says our own home-grown variety can change size at will. One moment they may be giants, the next minuscule folk who can readily be housed under a couple of rocks in the back yard. Believe it? "Hum!"

That's our story and we're sticking to it!

Tom and Minnie Gray

Ira, Tom Gray's son, behind the log store and stopping house, taken about 1911

Tom Gray pioneered wild country near site of Rocky

Thomas M. (Tom) Gray was quite a character.

Not tall, but muscular with unusually large hands and a keen mind for turning a dime into a dollar.

He was a born trader, known to have traded a two-dollar shotgun for a calf, the calf for an old cow, the cow for a lame mare that produced top foals year after year. No kidding, this man knew how to make money!

Born in Ontario in 1861, Tom moved to North Dakota as a young man, married and had a family of twelve children, eight of whom survived his nomadic life-style. At the turn of the century, he left his eldest children in the States and came to Alberta with his wife, Minnie, and their youngest children: Jay, Ira, Eph and Tommy.

Tom was by no means indigent, arriving in Canada in 1906 with a large string of horses and ten thousand dollars in cash, a veritable fortune in those days.

He built a two-story house west of Bentley, near a quiet little spring in the Medicine Lodge Hills, which were later renamed the Sunset Hills.

Perhaps it was too quiet for Tom, because he pulled up stakes in 1907 and moved to wilder country, about six km west of present day Rocky Mountain House.

In those days, there was no bridge over the North Saskatchewan River, so the river had to be forded on horseback. There was no "Town of Rocky," no rail line, only a collection of tarpaper shacks and a post office called Prairie Grange in the area we know today as "Old Town."

Presumably, Tom imagined commerce would revolve around the abandoned trading post, Fort Rocky Mountain House, because he built a huge log stopping house about a kilometre west of the ruins.

Tom and Min Gray's home and store—circa 1910

On this site he established the first general store in the area. His patrons at the store were mostly Stoney people and prospectors hurrying to the Nordegg area in search of coal

One Christmas Tom and his wife, Minnie, prepared a feast for well over one hundred men, women and children of the Stoney Nation.

The area's newspaper, the *Echo*, also reported dances and other social events given at Tom and Minnie's home, and no one ever left hungry.

As previously mentioned, Tom was always buying, selling or trading, so it wasn't long before he owned a good many quarters of land on both sides of the North Saskatchewan River. As a result, many deeds still bear Tom Gray's name. Tom was generous to a fault, often lending money to neighbours, many of whom simply couldn't repay him during the depression.

In 1912 his friend, Jack Killick, was operating a store in Evarts, but due to the railway bypassing Evarts, Jack was having a difficult time making ends meet. Learning of this, Tom invited the Killicks to manage the store Tom had opened some years before on the west side of the river. Later, Killick operated a second store in one of Tom's buildings in Rocky's Old Town. Some time later, Jack moved his wares to the new Rocky Mountain House town site where he and Joe Cony owned and operated the popular string of "Killico Stores" on Main Street.

In the early 1900s, a death occurred in the neighbourhood, so Tom asked some C.N.R surveyors who were working in the area to survey a 1.06-acres slice of land off the northeast corner of his home quarter for a burial site. This pie-shaped piece of land—Tom's donation to the community—holds the first graves in Garth Cemetery.

Tom loved the West Country, for it held unlimited pasture for his large herd of Curly Hair Horses. He had one favourite bay mare which he rode everywhere and, after the railway bridge was built, Tom taught the horse to carry him across the bridge without shying at the sight and sound of the river hundreds of meters below.

When the river was running free of ice, Tom thought nothing of fording it. He knew where it ran fast and deep and where the water was shallow. Sometimes he crossed the river on a horse. Other times he crossed it on foot, steadying himself with a pole. This was dangerous, to say the least, and may have led to his death.

As Tom and Minnie grew older, they began to travel to the States to see their children and several winters were spent in California with their daughter, Lorena. However, when Minnie's health failed their travels ended, and they were forced to move to Old Town and board with Mrs. Simms, a lady who took care of elderly folks for pay.

Tom hated living in town and longed for the wide-open spaces. At 80 years old, he was still in good health and, with the aide of an ivory-topped cane, felt confident to wander the country.

In the spring of 1941, forest fires were burning south of town, causing Tom to worry about the Simons family who lived on one of his quarters on the south side of the river.

From stories pieced together after Tom went missing, it appears he may have gone to visit them. At any rate, he never returned.

Footprints, believed to be Tom's, led through the freshly ploughed field and down to the river's edge. Family and neighbours joined police in an extensive search, but strangely, no trace of Tom, or his ivory-topped cane was ever found.

A medium predicts Tom's remains will eventually be found in an old well. Foul play? Who knows? Perhaps one day the mystery will be solved.

Mining towns tight-knit communities

In 2000 to 2004, I was coordinator-editor for the RMH-Nordegg area history book, *Days After Yesterday* and, as such, was extremely fortunate to collect stories from former residents of Alexo, Nordegg and Saunders.

Expecting statistics and a few fond memories to be unearthed when we put out the call for histories, I was totally unprepared for the emotion that tumbled out as folks spoke of life as it had been many years ago, in these once vibrant mining towns.

Perhaps this could well be called a true "saudade," when memories provoke such intense sad-sweetness the listener is moved to tears.

Ghost towns now, these three mining settlements had once been proud, self-contained communities where it was possible to be born, live an exciting life and be buried in one of the hillside cemeteries without ever seeing much of the "outside world."

Being geologically cut off from the rest of Alberta, these isolated towns fostered a neighbourly dependency and camaraderie not found elsewhere.

Yet remote as they were, the amenities of the mining towns were as good as, if not superior to any in Canada at that time, which was another reason the residents had such fierce pride in their towns. Mining camps were in evidence as early as 1899 when Saunders' first mines were recorded, precluding the town's official opening in 1913; Alexo opened in the early 20s, while Nordegg coalfields, discovered in 1911, led to 100 homes (all equipped with electricity) being built in 1914. Imagine electricity in miners' homes when most of Alberta's city dwellers were without power.

Coal was king in those days. Consequently, the three towns flourished and grew larger. In their heyday, each town had its own education and recreation facilities, and Nordegg had one of the most progressive hospitals in the province. Company stores carried a wide variety of groceries, clothing and hardware. There were hotels and churches; fairs and rodeos; hockey and ball teams; tennis courts and curling rinks; town bands and libraries.

The miners and their families worked hard and played hard. They laughed and cried together, birthed their babies and buried their loved ones. Some deaths came from natural causes, others from horrendous mine disasters. Through thick and thin, people pulled together, forging strong bonds and nurturing a lifestyle in hometowns they imagined would endure forever. Then the unthinkable happened in 1954-55—the mines closed.

Suddenly, the world slid away as three company-owned towns died and friends and families parted. For long-time residents closure was a shock of immense proportions, extremely difficult to cope with and impossible to forget. Many folks licked their wounds and went on to bigger and better careers; a few took their own lives.

Nordegg, now a tourist facility with exhibits of past glory days, recently gained status as a National Historic Site, and former residents of all three towns hold annual reunions.

In future columns I'd like to return to my file box, and with permission from former residents of Nordegg, Saunders and Alexo, share some individual memories of life in these once great mining towns.

Fond Memories of a ghost town

Have you ever been to a ghost town and imagined what life must have been like for the residents who lived there?

Many folks were raised in Alberta towns that no longer exist. Similar to us, these folks took their schooling, enjoyed sports, made friends, and then in a blink of an eye, their beloved hometown vanished. One such town was Alexo, a mining town, situated about a hundred miles due west of Red Deer.

One sunny autumn day—forty plus years ago—my husband, myself and our little ones went for a Sunday drive to Nordegg, and on the way back we stopped in at Alexo. This was ten years after the company-owned houses had been sold and moved to new locations, so the town that had been "home" to over 160 men, women and children was truly a thing of the past.

The one remaining building was the mine manager's home, which stood as a proud testament to Alexo's glory days. At the time of our visit, we were living in a very tiny house, so naturally I was totally captivated by this spacious two-storey home, which once hosted foreign diplomats and Alexo's high society.

"Oh, to live in a house such as this!" I remarked as we entered through a front door that former sightseers had left ajar. Even with piles of rubble on the hardwood floors, a squirrel's cache of dried mushrooms tucked in a corner and the acrid scent of pack rats, the house still held a sense of grandeur. There were five bedrooms—three up and two down—a modern bathroom, two kitchens (the outer kitchen once used on hot summer days), a sunlit dining room and sitting room with a large rock fireplace. It boggled my mind how such a home could be deserted, especially when I learned a little of Alexo's history.

William Andersen, mine manager, named the town after his former employer, Alexo Kelso, an Ontario mine owner. Andersen was quite an entrepreneur in his own right. Not only was he responsible for incorporating the Alexo Mining Company in May, 1920 and shipping Alexo's first coal in January 1921, but the main part of the beautiful mine manager's home was built to his specifications.

Unfortunately, William's chair in front of the homey fireplace was soon empty when he died suddenly, right there in Alexo in November 1921. Other mine managers came and went. The house was enlarged; the property landscaped with flowerbeds, lush lawns, neatly trimmed caragana hedges and white picket fences. A path from the house led under a trellis and up the hill to a tennis court. A breathtaking view of the Rocky Mountains could be seen from westerly windows, and below lay the mining town, complete with railway station, miner's homes, a school, a sprawling bunkhouse for single men, a hotel, general store and various mining buildings such as offices, a tipple and power and hoist buildings. One building housed a show hall, poolroom and doctor's quarters.

When we visited Alexo, the town was non-existent, and only the manager's house stood sentry over a valley pockmarked with cellar holes and broken foundations. The remains of a flagpole and fountain were still visible in the front yard, while forlorn-looking caraganas, delphiniums and poppies made their last stand among a tangle of weeds. Shortly after, we learned the grand old house was burned to the ground by the Department of Lands and Forest as it was considered a fire hazard and threat to the environment.

William Lees, war veteran, back home on the farm

Horrors of war hit home for vet's daughter

You wouldn't know him! Very few people did.

William Lees was a shy man, not someone you'd call a "mover and shaker."

In his quiet way, he helped build roads, a community hall and schoolhouse, and neighbours regularly called on him for assistance.

Some folks called him "Billy; most called him "Will". Regardless, he appeared to be just another green Englishman who filed on a homestead and spent 50 uneventful years, working mostly with horse-drawn equipment.

Yet, if his life in Central Alberta seemed drab, that had not always been the case. Will had a grisly past.

Will's childhood, spent in the seaside village of Southport, England, was pleasant enough. The nooks and crannies of the large house where he was born made excellent places to play.

Will excelled at map-making in school and enjoyed family walks to Blowick Station to watch the trains shunt back and forth. In a nearby park he saw the world's first airplanes make unsuccessful attempts to liftoff. Life was good until Will's father bought a one-way ticket to New Zealand and his mother died.

In 1912, when Will was eighteen and head of the household, he brought his brother and sister to Canada.

He arrived in Calgary with 50 cents in his pocket. Two years later, when the First World War broke out, he was working near Ponoka for W.L. Gee, earning money to pay for brother John's schooling.

Much to Will's dismay, after graduating as a teacher from Camrose Normal, John joined the army. Will's conscience wouldn't allow him to sit idly by while his younger brother was fighting in France, so he, too, joined up and was sent overseas in March 1917.

This was the month of the heaviest shipping losses in the war, and the troop transport, carrying Will and his regiment, had to dodge German submarines while making the ocean crossing.

Once in France, Will was stationed near Vimy Ridge where exploding shells had riddled the countryside with craters, and booted feet still protruded from collapsed trenches.

Will's first duty was cleaning the trenches—and when lunch had to be eaten beside the decaying bodies of dead soldiers, he felt too nauseated to eat. Shortly after this, Will received word his brother's battalion, the 46th, was located nearby, so he decided to pay the young lad a visit, only to find he'd been killed a few days before. One can only imagine the horror Will experienced on hearing the news and seeing the fresh mound in a French cemetery.

The next two months were spent cleaning trenches and packing supplies, then in August 1917, Will joined the 50th Battalion for active duty on the front line.

Will said, "The second day out was sticky and hot, and the sky was pitch black. Then enemy guns opened up with a mixture of whizz-bangs and gas shells. A cloud of mist dropped over the trenches and we scrambled to pull on our gas masks. This was my first brush with death—the first and last time I was actually terrified during the entire war."

However, there were many more "close-calls" when men beside Will were blown to pieces. Will joined a special "tump line" unit to pack supplies to the front, balancing on slippery planks above shell holes so full of water, that men, who fell into them, drowned. Of the original 12 "tump-liners," only Will and three others survived. There were nights of carrying stretchers and helping the walking wounded to safety, followed by burying fallen comrades. It was hell!

Beside human carnage, the area was strewn with the mutilated bodies of mules and horses. Will recalled seeing one of the last wartime cavalry charges. He said, "I heard the commander yell, 'Forward,' and saw the horses gallop down a hill into a volley of machinegun fire. Within seconds the whole detachment was transformed into a pile of flailing hooves and bloody corpses."

It's hard to imagine the horrors of war, day in and day out. Adding to the trauma, Will voluntarily joined a Canadian machinegun corps.

Canadian Machinegun Corps:—taken January 1919 at Troisdorf, Germany. Wm. Lees is second from right, fifth row from the back.

This was extremely dangerous because if the allies retreated, machine-gunners had to hold their positions to allow ground troops to draw back; consequently, machine-gunners seldom survived an enemy advance.

The war raged on, and Will was in the thick of the battle. Then on November 11, 1918, armistice was declared amid much cheering and celebrating. Next Will took part in the victory march through France, Belgium and Germany, marching an average of 25 kilometres daily, often under fire from enemy snipers who refused to concede defeat. Here, Will salvaged six live German shells as souvenirs—two for himself and four for his buddies—disengaging the highly explosive mechanisms with his jackknife.

Later, Will marched in front of Buckingham Palace before King George, Queen Mary and future prime minister, Winston Churchill. Again there was wild cheering and people yelling, "We're proud of you, Canada!"

After that Will returned to the homestead where he spent the next half century struggling to make ends meet as a farmer, logger and postmaster.

Who would have guessed this modest man had endured so much in the line of duty. As his daughter, it took me many years to fully appreciate his wartime contributions.

Yet, today as I visit his grave, I say a special thanks to the many Canadian war heroes similar to my dad, who fought and continue to fight for freedom.

Memories of Christmas from the past

December's here, and as the snow begins to cover rooftops each of us regardless of age, engage in a common activity—we find ourselves glancing in the rear view mirror, so to speak, and remembering past Christmases.

My special Christmas memory revolves around the year when I was seven, and caught up, as most children are, in dreams of toys and candy.

This particular year, I had something special to look forward to. My two sisters and I had asked Santa to bring a new baby brother to our house, and for all intents and purposes (our mother was growing chubbier by the day), it appeared that dear old Santa was set to deliver.

Excitement reined supreme at our house as we anticipated the blessed event. Then, a few days before Christmas, Mother became seriously ill, and we children watched in horror as she disappeared on a dark wintry night, en-route to the Rocky Mountain House Hospital.

Since our parents had immigrated to Canada—alone—we had no extended family to assist in this type of emergency, a sad state of affairs, especially at Christmas when the neighbours were all very busy preparing their own family celebrations.

The evening Mother was admitted to hospital happened to be the night of our school Christmas concert, and the teacher of our one-room school gave me a tiny book entitled, *Star of the King*, a child's version of the birth of Jesus.

I read this little book over and over, and the story was remarkably comforting.

And then something quite amazing happened. The two busiest "moms" in the district took us under their wing. One of the women, Beryl Robinson had eight children; the other, Katherine Cornforth, had thirteen.

Can you imagine these two hardworking ladies welcoming more children into their already crowded homes, making extra beds and sharing meals during their busiest time of year? Talk about Christmas Spirit!

There were families with fewer children and larger homes in the community who might have offered to take us in, but didn't. Yet, these two women with the least resources made room in their hearts and homes for three frightened little girls.

On Christmas Eve, Father came home saying, "Santa won't be bringing a baby to our house this year." However, Mother was rallying and would be home soon. Great news!

So, we settled down to a "no fuss" Christmas with a few small gifts wrapped in brown paper under a sparsely decorated tree, eating whenever we felt like it (mostly toast and jam) and spending no time at all on housework.

Which makes me wonder why today's housewives run themselves ragged preparing for Christmas.

Certainly we three girls enjoyed a very simple Christmas that year, content in the knowledge our mother was recovering and richly blessed by visits to the homes of those two caring neighbours.

Although Katherine and Beryl have long since passed away, their many descendants are scattered across Canada. Some make their home in Central Alberta and still practice the values they were taught, treating their neighbours with love, respect and a helping hand.

As a seven year-old, I learned an important lesson from those two benevolent neighbours: expensive Christmas gifts and grandiose parties are seldom memorable, yet when good-hearted people reach out to those in need, Christmas becomes a season to remember.

Following a very traumatic Christmas, life returned to normal with Mother, elder sister, Evelyne and younger sister, Doreen.

1907
MARKERVILLE LUTHERAN CHURCH

Markerville church springs to life at Christmas

Starry nights, crunching snow, church bells and luminaries. It is the spirit of Christmas that brings people flocking to the Christmas Eve Service held each year in the Markerville Lutheran Church.

As they have done for an even 100 years, friends and neighbours of all denominations gather here at seven o'clock to sit in hinged wooden seats, blend their voices in ancient carols and listen to the story of the Christ Child as told in children's skits, Bible readings and musical selections.

Hark the Harold Angels Sing!

On such a night as this, the words of the carol take on new meaning, for surely the angels have visited this little church in the smiling faces of these good neighbours, shaking hands, hugging and wishing each other peace and joy throughout this festive season.

Indeed this warm friendly spirit never leaves Markerville. Nestled on the banks of the Medicine River, the settlement dates back to 1888, when a colony of Icelanders took up permanent residence in the area.

The church itself was built in 1907 and rededicated this past summer for the church's centennial.

Originally constructed as a Lutheran Church, it is not open on a regular basis, but the large white doors open for special seasonal services and the occasional wedding or funeral.

It also serves as an attraction for tourists each summer who flock to the heart of the community—the Historic Markerville Creamery Museum.

The Museum, which was declared an historic site in 1974, was a working creamery serving the farmers in the community for seventy-three years from 1899 to 1972.

Now it operates as a very modern museum, endorsing the concepts of "showing, rather than telling."

You will not find many items behind glass here. Summer visitors are treated to a delightful tour, seeing first hand the authentic models of butter making and pasteurizing equipment used in yesteryear.

The Creamery Museum is operated under the auspices of the community based Stephan G. Stephansson Icelandic Society.

Besides offering walk-through tours and educational school programs, the museum hosts a variety of special events and, during the summer, mans a coffee shop where hungry visitors are treated to Icelandic delicacies.

A measure of the museums success can be seen in the 15,000 tourists it attracts annually, with many return visitors.

Although the tourist season is limited to six months, from May 15th to Labour Day, there are other activities during the winter months, such as coffee at 10 am, daily, for anyone who cares to drops in.

There are semi-monthly whist drives, Winterfest in February and Christmas in Markerville in November.

As well there are potluck suppers and money making events where neighbours come en masse to enjoy homemade food and good company. A camp ground, located on the banks of the Medicine River, gives summer visitors a quiet place to relax, either as picnickers or overnight campers.

Summer or winter, Markerville seems always at peace, both in its setting and in the old-fashioned neighbourly atmosphere which prevails here. "Oh little town of Markerville how still we see thee lie," a true oasis in a busy world—a place where neighbours care for neighbours, and the Christmas spirit abides 365 days of the year.

Above is Red Deer's
Berkhamsted Farm,

Left: Dr. Thomas Fry

Agricultural training school largely forgotten

Have you ever heard of Red Deer's Berkhamsted Farm? Very few people have, yet the story behind the name is quite intriguing.

Berkhamsted Farm was Alberta's first agricultural school. It was an ancillary of the prestigious English Berkhamsted Grammar School—a school established for boys in Britain in 1541 and girls in 1888. Still in operation in England today, Berkhamsted Collegiate School is attended by young people from all parts of the globe and boasts such famous students as Clementine Churchill and Graham Greene.

Getting back to Red Deer's Berkhamsted School, this venture was the brainchild of Dr. Thomas Fry, a former headmaster of the English Berkhamsted School and, like all dreamers, Fry fully expected his school on the outskirts of Red Deer to operate forever, which may have been the case had it not been for the outbreak of the First World War.

While touring the States and Canada in 1900, looking for the ideal spot to set up his agricultural training facility, Fry happened to stop in Red Deer to visit one of his "old boys," young mister Simpson. Simpson was homesteading a quarter of 2-38-27-W5 and, having tired of pioneer life, it took little persuasion to sell his land to the doctor. Fry then bought a block of six more quarters—the remainder of section two, and south-half and NE-11-38-27-W5th.

In all, Fry wound up with a total of 1,120 acres before having a contractor build a two-story house on the newly acquired property. The house was considered large for the times. With 139 square meters (1,500 sq. ft) of living space on each floor, it held a living room, dining room, kitchen, washroom and smoking room on the main floor. Upstairs was an office, two spare bedrooms and a room with eight dorm-sized cubicles to house students.

Next, Fry selected the most industrious young men from the mother school. After paying their own passage, the young males were expected to spend two years working at Red Deer's Berkhamsted Farm for little or no wages while training to become Alberta farmers. Initially the young Englishmen, with their delicate accents and gentlemanly conduct, were considered sissies by those born in the Wild West. Consequently Fry's facility was dubbed "the baby school."

There was also a great deal of speculation as to what the school was qualified to teach, for Fry didn't possess much in the way of agricultural savvy. For instance, one spring the doctor insisted on helping friends weed their garden and yanked up an entire row of young cabbage plants, leaving in their place a healthy row of weeds.

Despite the jokes fielded at the school's occupants, the school was a no-nonsense, no-frills facility designed to condition young men for the worst scenarios—and that it did. Graduates of Red Deer's Berkhamsted School were said to be able to endure endless hardship.

A case in point was a young Englishman by the name of George Randoph Pearkes, who came to the Red Deer Farm in 1906. After completing a two-year stint at the school, George filed on a homestead on the west side of the Clearwater River. Here he single-handedly built a one-room log cabin that gave new meaning to the word "rustic" for its unchinked walls allowed wind, rain and snow an unhampered passage to the interior. Packing boxes served as chairs, and George's bed was a bundle of spruce bows on a high spot on the dirt floor.

No need to laugh; Bob Ross (for whom Mt. Ross is named) built George a decent house which became home until George joined the RCMP in 1912. Then, with the coming of war, George, along with other Berkhamsted boys, joined up. 1915 found them in France where George was wounded in the battle of Passchendale. In spite of suffering from severe injuries, George continued to lead his men. For this and other unselfish acts, George was awarded the Victoria Cross. In the Second World War, he and Lionel Page, another former Red Deer Berkhamsted student, became Major-Generals. Both were awarded the DSO (Distinguished Service Order) and Bar.

Major-General George Pearkes then went on to become the Federal Minister of Defense under Prime Minister Diefenbaker's Tories. Later, he served as the Lieutenant Governor of British Columbia from 1960-68.

Not a bad record for young men educated in Red Deer Unfortunately many other Berkhamsted boys lost their lives in the First World War.

Frank and Leonard Patterson, both students of Berkhamsted Farm School, enlisted. Leonard was wounded twice and his kid brother, Leaman, and brother-in-law, Frank Holt—both English born recruits in the Canadian Armed Forces—were killed in action.

Frank and Leonard Patterson are thought to be the only students of Red Deer's Berkhamsted School to make a permanent home in Central Alberta. Frank lived in the Alhambra area and served as Justice of the Peace, while his brother Ralph Patterson was well known as secretary-manager for the Red Deer Fair.

"What became of Red Deer's Berkhamsted agricultural school?" you ask.

The school operated full bore for about ten years before being phased out during the First World War. When the school closed, Dr Fry hired the Eversole family, immigrants from the mid-west United States, to manage the farm on shares.

Canon Charles Fry, an amiable clergyman, inherited the farm after his father and brother's death.

Charles owned and often visited the farm until 1947 when the historic Berkhamsted Farm was broken into four units and sold, 240 acres going to its former managers, John and Gertrude Eversole who were known far and wide for their excellent farming practices.

Today, Red Deer's "Berkhamsted Farm," the first agricultural based school in Alberta, is relatively unknown. Occupying part of the old farmland are the new housing developments of Vanier Woods and Lancaster Meadows.

Let’s not forget the Bayly boys’ contribution

In an earlier column on Red Deer’s Berkhamsted School, I omitted to mention another family linked with the school.

In recording the history of Central Alberta, we often overlook folks who made significant contributions to our community and then moved on.

Typical of early contributors were the Bayly brothers, Edwin, Herbert, Gilbert and Vincent, who in 1906 set up a ranch on the banks of the Clearwater River, 16 km (ten miles) south of present day Rocky Mountain House.

All four boys were educated in the prestigious Berkhamsted School in England, which I mentioned in an earlier column.

Instead of attending University (a family tradition), the Bayly boys followed their English headmaster’s advice and immigrated to Alberta with dreams of building impressive estates. At the time, their former headmaster, Dr. Fry, owned Berkhamsted Farm in Red Deer, an agricultural school designed to teach young Englishmen the intricacies of farming in Central Alberta.

The country west of Red Deer was predominantly muskegs and mosquitoes in 1906 when sixteen-year-old Vincent Bayly and his older brothers moved to their new homestead.

Herbert Bayly's home built in 1906-07 on the Clearwater Ranch, eight miles south of Rocky Mountain House .

There were no bridges spanning either the Clearwater or North Saskatchewan Rivers. Consequently the most accessible town was Innisfail. This in turn meant traveling by horse, 80 km (fifty miles) over hills, creeks and swampland to get mail, groceries and building supplies.

The boys hung a sign, Clearwater Ranch, on the entrance to their section of land and set about building two-story homes which were quite ornate for the times.

Although Herbert (Bertie) had no formal carpentry training, he was the master builder and, after four homes were built, the young men were joined by their parents and sister, Alice.

Edwin, Gilbert, Bertie, Vincent, Alice, Agnes & Herbert Bayly at Clearwater Ranch

For the Bayly women, adapting to pioneer life was quite a shock, especially the first cold winter when wind whistled through cracks in log walls and woodstoves filled the rooms with smoke.

Come spring, the women scratched out vegetable and flower gardens while the men folk cleared as much land as they could to plant oats and barley. From their doorsteps, they had a spectacular view of the Clearwater River and snow-capped Rocky Mountains forty miles to the west, and now and then caught sight of coyotes, bears, moose, elk or deer. Every experience was new and exciting.

On hot summer days the family swam in the river and enjoyed formal outdoor picnics with other homesteaders. In fact, the Baylys had quite a social life, hosting dances and house parties. Some evenings their young bachelor friend, George Pearkes (later a Victoria Cross recipient and B.C.'s Lieutenant Governor) arrived to recite poetry.

Even Anglican Church services were held in the Bayly homes. Proposing to build an Anglican church, a meeting was called in Leslieville on Dec. 2, 1911.

All five of the Bayly men attended and offered to donate land for the church. Although a church didn't materialize at that time, the meeting sewed the seeds for future development. Holy Trinity Anglican Church was built in Rocky in 1929, and in 1948, All Hallows Anglican Church was built in the Chedderville area, a few miles south of Baylys' Ranch.

As census taker, Bertie Bayly rode his horse down frozen rivers to collect names of local residents—records which are still in use today. Romance also kept Bertie in the saddle, riding back and forth to Innisfail Post Office.

He was corresponding with Gladys Gordon, a feisty young lady who attended Berkhamsted Girls' School in the old country. Then in 1911 he hopped an eastbound train and married Gladys as soon as her ship docked in Montreal.

She was a beautiful girl—the only Bayly female truly suited for pioneer life. Born on a farm in South Africa, she loved the outdoors, milked cows, operated the horse-drawn binder at harvest time, the plow in the spring, chinked her log home and picked and canned wild fruit.

Gladys was also an excellent rider, and in 1912 she won top prize for horsemanship in the first Rocky Mountain House Agricultural Fair. Later that year Gladys and Bertie's daughter, Beryl, was born in Innisfail.

Had it not been for World War I, the Bayly family may have remained on the Clearwater Ranch. However, similar to other Berkhamsted boys, Edwin and Vincent Bayly joined the army in 1915. Gilbert moved to Ottawa and became a Dominion Land Surveyor, while the remaining family moved to B.C. Then, in 1919, Bertie and his young family moved permanently to Gladys's childhood home in South Africa—and so the Baylys' stay in Alberta officially ended.

"The Vines," Bertie and Glady Baylys' home in South Africa

No relatives remain to boast of their accomplishments, but certainly the family left something of themselves behind. Over the years, their Alberta homes, built with such care, housed many other settlers, while land the Bayly boys broke with little more than their bare hands is still being farmed today.

As well, social activities they helped organize provided a foundation for our own cultural development. Regardless of their length of stay in Alberta, it's fitting to acknowledge early residents, such as these fine young men who played an important part in carving a wilderness into civilization.

Romance, tragedy and adventure

"Hey, Look at that," my husband said as he pointed to a truck with an Alberta license plate. "It's Big Horn Transport!"

Now seeing a truck with the Big Horn decal on its door might be a common sight in Central Alberta, but we weren't in Alberta when we saw this particular truck. We were driving Arizona's I-10, near the Mexican border, and certainly weren't expecting to see such a familiar trucking outfit this far from home.

Watching the truck disappear in our rearview mirror brought to mind the story behind the Big Horn Transport—an intriguing tale of romance and sorrow, hardship and outstanding fortitude.

The story began in 1910 in Italy when 24-year-old Andrea (Andrew) Blasetti decided to follow in his brother's footsteps and sail to the Americas. The States and Canada held great promise in the early 1900s, and Andrew was certain he could do well in the new world. However, there was one undeniable glitch. He'd fallen in love with a young lady by the name of Bernardina Serani and wasn't anxious to leave her. Chances were, he'd be gone a long time, and what if Bernardina forgot him while he was in some faraway land, attempting to make his fortune? Gathering up his courage, he proposed marriage, and when she accepted, he and Bernardina were married in Antrodoco, their hometown. Then, after only one month of married life, the groom sailed away. Andrew was 24 years old, Bernardina was 22, and it would be two long years before the newlyweds were together again.

After a short stay in New York, Andrew worked in the undersea coal mines of Nova Scotia, then on to Calgary where he worked on road crews and in Burn's meat packing plant.

Finally he saved enough money for Bernardina's fare, and what a happy day it was when she arrived in Calgary in 1912. However, their happiness was marred by financial woes, so when Brazeau Colliers opened a coal mine in Nordegg, Andrew was among the first miners to leave for the mine.

Once again Bernardina found herself alone, this time in Calgary where baby Guido was born in 1913. For the young Italian mother, living in an English speaking city was difficult, and she longed to be with her husband. So, one day she packed nine-month old Guido to the railway station, climbed into a boxcar and made the long trip to Nordegg. It was a most uncomfortable journey, seated on the floor of a boxcar, nursing her baby—the only woman—surrounded by workmen going to the mines.

Tired and hungry, she arrived in Nordegg only to discover there were no accommodations for women, only bunk houses for working men. So, young Mrs. Blasetti and her family made their home in a tent until a house was built several months later. The following year, Guido's brother, Ernest, became the first non-native child born in Nordegg and in coming years, four more children joined the family: Mary, Evo, Mafalda and Frank.

Time passed. Andrew continued working in the mines. Bernardina picked berries, raised chickens, grew a large garden and supplemented the family income by selling bread to bachelors and laundering miners' clothes.

In subsequent years, Nordegg grew into a thriving town with all the amenities of city living. Yet with Mount Coliseum and Mount Baldy keeping watch over the rows of company-owned houses, the town had an unspoiled, natural beauty not found in a city.

There were shops, churches, social clubs, indoor plumbing and electricity—and best of all, a wonderful camaraderie found nowhere else.

The Andrew Blasetti family: (top left) Guido, whose brothers Frank (top right) and Ernest (lower right) died in separate coal mine accidents in Nordegg

It seemed life couldn't be better; the Blasettis were realizing their fondest dreams. That was, until tragedy struck Oct. 31, 1941. Children were in high spirits that Halloween afternoon, getting ready to go trick or treating, when the mine's steam whistle blew, alerting those above ground of a mine explosion. All too soon news came that twenty-nine miners had lost their lives. Andrew and Bernardina knew all of the victims, for they were close friends and neighbours. Yet, a greater heartbreak lay in store on June 2 1947, when their youngest son, Frank, was killed in a mine cave-in. Then, February 9, 1949, their second son, Ernest, was crushed to death by a runaway mine car.

Rather than work in the mines, Guido, the son who had come to Nordegg in a box car as an infant, decided to go into business for himself. And in 1947, after a stint in the Navy and several less appealing business ventures, he officially registered his new trucking operation, naming it Big Horn Transport Ltd.

Earlier, in 1941, Guido had eloped with his childhood sweetheart, Julia Poscente. Now, as man and wife, he and Julia worked hard, building the transport business while raising three daughters and six sons. A new 1947, 3-ton Mercury truck was purchased from Hepworth Motors in Red Deer, and a van was constructed using wood for the frame, covered by sheets of galvanized corrugated metal.

After Leduc's oil strike in 1947 and Nordegg's catastrophic fire at the Bazeau Colliers in 1950, Guido predicted the inevitable: Nordegg's boom days were coming to an end. With this in mind, he moved his family and transport company to Red Deer in 1953. Then in 1957, the head office was moved from Red Deer to Calgary and the family owned business grew in leaps and bounds. Through good times and bad, the work ethics Guido's parents taught him kept him focused, and eventually all six sons joined him in the transport business.

Prior to his death in 2001, Guido was presented with a prestigious, historical award from the Alberta Trucking Association for his 50 years of service in the field of transportation.

This past summer The Big Horn Transport celebrated its 60th year of operation with third and fourth generations of the Blasetti family actively involved in the business. The company, which started from such humble beginnings, now operates from terminals in Edmonton, Calgary, Lethbridge and Regina. Its fleet of 110 tractors and 580 trailers can be seen on any given day hauling freight across Western Canada. The transports also make runs to the Artic in the north, and—as we discovered—to southern states.

As for the Blasettis themselves, they have become a huge family, yet they have never forgotten their roots. Every August they travel back to Nordegg to enjoy a giant family camp-out. At 94 years of age, Julia Blasetti is still the family's central figure and bakes 20 to 25 pies at a time to feed her ever expanding family. She also directs an annual work bee in which 500 kg (1,100 pounds) of tomatoes and 135 (300 pounds) of celery are used in the family's favorite recipe—Italian sauce.

How could Andrew and Bernardina possibly suspect, when they left Italy so many years ago, that they were writing the first page of one of Alberta's greatest success stories?

Big sister and I.
Do we look like the kind of kids who'd set fire to the granary and chicken house pictured below?

The day we burned the hay shed down

Time! How fast it goes!

Yesterday is only a blink away, a flicker of an eyelash. Yet we are always trying to recapture our yesterdays, trying to reconstruct them, understand them, if not garnish them with rose-coloured adjectives. Embellishment is especially true if those "yesterdays" belonged to our late-great ancestors. We tend to knead their lives into sugary little appetizers to suit our taste. Why not? The dearly departed aren't here to correct us.

Looking ahead, say a hundred years from today, we can readily imagine our descendants trying to get a handle on how we lived our lives, yet they may have a hard time putting a realistic slant on our activities, mainly because the past century has been an era of phenomenal changes in Alberta's life-styles.

For myself, life began in the Aurora district north of Leslieville, where my immigrant parents chose to settle. At the time of my birth there was no electricity, no indoor plumbing, no motorized vehicles. The shack we lived in had none of the modern amenities we later became accustomed to—the ones our kids take for granted.

I can still picture the hole in the floor of my first home—a hole drilled by former tenants to drain rainwater from the kitchen when the roof leaked. There was plenty of venison as well as wild berries back then, providing sustenance for us wilderness people who likely would have starved to death without Mother Nature's benevolence.

Having the innocence of youth was a great blessing, for we three sisters never felt anything but secure in our little home. We didn't know how many times our parents were penniless, nor were we aware that the morning porridge was served, not always by choice, but necessity. Oatmeal was cheap and nutritious and when our hens were laying, we ate eggs—lots of them—and drank milk when the cows freshened.

Now if our kids think this was a ho-hum existence, it wasn't. We made our own entertainment, loved excitement and, every now and then, flirted with real danger. A case in point was the time my sister and I set fire to the hay shed. This was in the spring of the year, early '40s, when Father and Mother were listening to a crystal set, a contraption with headphones which brought in radio waves. We couldn't afford a real radio. I was all of three and a half; my sister, seven.

Mother kept matches on the very top of a makeshift cupboard: six wooden apple crates nailed one on top of the other with a curtain covering the gaping end.

I held the homemade stool my sister teetered on while she grabbed a handful of matches. Then out we scooted behind the chicken coop to smoke. Of course, we had no real cigarettes, so we were in the habit of finding plump barley straws to suck in the smoke—like we'd seen our father doing with his cigarettes.

Behind the chicken coop was a hay shed, and curiosity took us to the brown hen nesting there. The eggs were hatching, so we admired the new chicks before lighting up. We'd played this smoking game before, but never in such volatile surroundings.

The memory is as plain as day: me seated on top of a pile of hay, watching a straw burn and dropping it when it scorched my fingers. Woosh! Immediately the hay around us caught fire. How we escaped death is a mystery.

"Where are you going with that water?" Father asked, as my sister scooped up a dipperful of drinking water from a pail in the kitchen.

"The chickens are thirsty," she called back, but there was no putting out a large blaze with a few dribbles of water, so she was soon racing to the house to tell our unsuspecting parents the hay shed was on fire. By this time the roofs of the chicken coop and a nearby granary were smouldering and, had it not been for a bucket brigade formed by neighbours, all our farm buildings would have gone up in flames. As it was only the hay shed was lost and—much to my horror—the baby chicks.

Do these type of early beginnings shape who we are?

Were important lessons learned at an early age when money was scarce, when radios and TVs were non-existent, when fire burned baby birds and neighbours came together in emergencies?

Did life in Alberta in the early 40s foster a unique kind of appreciation for life?

I think so.

Above is the first Big Horn School. Today's modern school is below.

Pictured below is a small portion of the beautiful Big Horn Reserve

A colourful past for the West Country

Looking back at the history of our west country, I can't help but think of some very special folks, the First Nation families who live in the valley of the mighty Big Horn River.

The Big Horn Reserve was officially established in 1948 by seven Stoney families from the Morley Reserve: the Abraham, Beaver, Dixon, House, Poucette, Wesley and Wildman families. Situated 32 km (20 miles) west of Nordegg, the reserve appears to be a recent entity in the history of the break-away band, yet in reality it isn't. This magnificent river valley with its clear, rushing water and towering mountains was home to Stoneys long before boundaries of a reserve were laid out.

Mary Schaffer, the famous female Philadelphia explorer/photographer, made several expeditions from 1889 to 1911 into the Canadian Rockies, and told of her visits to the families of Silas Abraham (for whom Lake Abraham is named) and Paul and Samson Beaver who were camped on the Kootenay Plains near the confluence of the North Saskatchewan and Big Horn Rivers.

Unfamiliar with the mountains to the north, Schaffer was delighted when Samson Beaver drew a map for her party to follow. Later, as Schaffer scanned the rocky crags rising up from Maligne Lake, she named a majestic 940 meter (3,081 ft.) mountain, Samson Peak, after the map-maker.

Intrigued by the beauty of the land, Mary wrote, "There is no describing the Kootenai Plains. To appreciate them one must let the soft winds caress the face and allow the eye to absorb the blue of the surrounding hills and the gold of the grasses beneath the feet. To see the plains at their best, one should come over Pipestone in August and look down on the scene from the rolling hills to the south. Then the golden-brown of the ripened grasses flood the valley with light. For miles the river winds and twists from west to east. An occasional Indian shack comes to view. The faint ringing of a bell denotes that a few tiny specks on the landscape are really horses and the white dots are tepees of the Indians. No wonder the Indians from Morley come here year after year; I only wonder that the whole tribe does not attempt to move in one body."

Yet the Stoneys of Montana's Assiniboin race who spoke various dialects of Dakota (or Nakota), weren't ready to settle in one place in 1889. They were perfectly happy to wander, as they had done for centuries before, following game trails and gathering edible plants and berries when and where the changing seasons provided them. Nor were they ready to settle down when Grandpa Tom Gray first made their acquaintance in 1907.

Tom had built a store and stopping house on the west side of the North Saskatchewan River near the site of the deserted Hudson Bay Fort. The Stoneys used to camp near the store for several days at a time while they made their purchases of tea, flour, tobacco and other staples, and Tom enjoyed telling of Christmas 1916 when over a hundred Stoney men, women and children were dinner guests at his home. Stoney elder, Norman Abraham, also told of these celebrations.

"We used to go to Tom Gray's store, and old Tom

would dance all night," Norman said, laughing heartily as he recalled the days of his youth.

After the Big Horn Reserve was formed in '48, the residents were known as the Wesley Band after their leader, Peter Wesley Sr., whom they called *The Great Taotha.* Peter Wesley was a venerable leader, but not a chief. The Big Horn has never had a resident chief, since the Wesley Band's affairs are administrated in Morley. However, the Big Horn elders select their own counselor, and a recent counselor was John Wesley, grandson of Peter Wesley Sr.

One of the first permanent buildings to be constructed on the reserve in 1948-49 was a log schoolhouse. This was built by Peter Wesley Jr. and his son, John. Recreation was also an integral part of reserve life: ball games, horseback riding, and as soon as ice formed on the river, the boys played hockey.

Girls skated too, but they were expected to wear dresses until the early sixties when a change in policy allowed females to wear jeans and shorts if they choose to.

In the '40s and '50s the Wesley Band participated in Nordegg's sports days and parades.

One former Nordegg resident recalls,"The Stoney Indians made a very colourful entry to these events, coming in full traditional regalia, feathered headdresses and beautifully beaded vests, leggings and moccasins. And they always invited Nordegg folks back to 'Big Horn Days,' which is the name of the annual native rodeo."

Until Nordegg mines closed in 1955, the men of the reserve worked in coal mines, then bush camps, and later helped build the David Thompson Highway.

In recent years, both men and women have branched out into challenging careers in many walks of life, such as the oil industry and social services. Today's Big Horn youth spend a great deal of time in hockey rinks and arenas all over Alberta, and a good many trophies grace kitchen cabinets on the Big horn Reserve, due to the young athletes' proficiency in sports.

When recording histories for *The Days After Yesterday*, the Rocky-Nordegg community history book, I was privileged to visit homes of the Big Horn families. Edna Penner who had lived on the reserve for over twenty years accompanied me, and we received a warm welcome wherever we went.

Edna and her late husband had been employed by the Federal Government as teachers, and Edna remembers those years as some of her happiest. Her daughters, Faith and Gloria, were raised with the Big Horn children and quite naturally learned to speak the Stoney language.

The Penners were also actively involved in the Big Horn Store and Service Station operated by the band. When Peter Penner died in 1999, his Stoney friends requested he be buried in the Big Horn Cemetery, an offer gratefully accepted by Peter's family.

Although population was slow to increase in the early years due to high infant mortality, today with improved health care facilities, more than 200 people make their home on the Big Horn Reserve. A religious Sun Dance is held at the summer solstice, and competitive native dances are held as separate events with young and old participating.

On a personal note, a new generation of Grays and Stoney people still enjoy each others' company—just as their great-great-grandfathers did so many years ago.

Taken in the 1940s, this photo shows Jenny Rabbit driving ahead, while husband, Norman Abraham, and passenger follow. They were likely travelling from the Kootenay Plains to the Stoney headquarters in Morley. Photo compliments of Sarah (Rabbit-Abraham) Schug

On special occasions, children living on the Big Horn Reserve dress in traditional costumes as they learn the songs and dances of their ancestors.

The elections the Grits won, then lost

With all the election hype in the country, there's one particular story which bears repeating—a melodrama of sorts that took place June 7, 1917, when Edward Michener, the Conservative candidate for Red Deer, ran against Liberal R.B. Wellever.

Excitement built as each candidate threw himself on the mercy of their constituents.

The tension, as is always the case, grew thin and brittle beforehand, but finally election day arrived, voters came, polls closed, ballots were counted and Wellever was declared the winner by a narrow majority.

In high spirits Wellever and his party-faithful hit the streets to celebrate after what appeared to be their rise to power.

A victory parade was staged on Gaetz Avenue with Liberals brandishing flaming brooms, which had previously been soaked in kerosene.

However, someone had neglected to tell Wellever that chickens should never be counted before they're actually hatched.

In those days, Red Deer Constituency took in a huge area to the west, and the contents of a ballot box from Strachan, a tiny community 30 km south of Rocky Mountain House, had not yet been tallied when Liberal celebrations got underway.

After being pelted with heavy rain all week, road conditions were horrific, and automobile travel was impossible in the Strachan area.

So a horseback rider was dispatched to deliver what everyone assumed would be a ballot box containing one or two ballots.

All through the night the dispatcher rode under dark, drizzling skies, over hills and through muskegs, 110 km all told.

When the ballot box was finally delivered to Red Deer, a new winner was declared—Edward Michener, by 23 votes.

How had such a small community tipped the balance of power?

The answer lay in the main election issue—conscription—supported by the Conservatives and opposed by the Liberals.

Many of Strachan's first homesteaders, such as former Berkhamsted School students mentioned in a previous column, were young Brits.

These young men were already in active service at the time of the 1917 provincial election, and it appears that parents, siblings and friends came out to show their support by voting.

There is a lesson for all of us in that scenario. Had it not been for this small Central Alberta farming community, Michener would not have been re-elected to the legislature.

His election paved the way for his appointment to the Senate in 1918, which in turn triggered moving his family to Toronto. The move precluded his son Roland's election to the House of Commons as Federal Minister of Defense in 1953 under the Diefenbaker administration.

Later, Roland Michener was Speaker of The House, before becoming Canada's Governor General.

In short, what appeared in 1917 to be an insignificant ballet box carried by horse and rider to Red Deer changed the course of history.

It's an election-day story which clearly shows how each and every vote counts and why we need to mark an X for the candidate of our choice come next election day.

Note: Strachan Post Office was the heart of the community The post office was first named Vetchland, because an abundance of wild vetch grew in the area. Later, the post office was named for David Gordon Strachan, a popular young man killed in the First World War. The following list of mail patrons is an indicator of the community's size.

1915-1917 Those receiving mail at Strachan were David Strachan, Frank Hayworth, Carlson McDonald, Bert Barkham, Joe Chambers, Charlie Apperson, John Pollock, Norman Scott, Bill Watkins, Mose Rundell, Jim Watts, Walter Dobbs, Charlie Crotchet, Pat Bolan, Joshua Jackson, Jack Bold and the families of Fred & Albert Parson, Frank & Mrs. Miel (Sr.), Elmer & S. A. Osborne, Wm, Sid & Fred Strong, Sid & Tom Milbank, John & Roy Severs, Bert Lea, Albert Pike, Harris Smith Jarrot, Graham, Hamelin, Odendal, Beagher, Sabler, Chesney and the Major boys.

Howard Thompson 1941

In 1999 Howard, age 80, completed the 100 km RCMP Centennial Ride on horseback from Red Deer to Rocky.

Interesting life of Howard Thompson

Some years ago I met a gentleman who had the most interesting stories to tell.

Since he always spoke of other folks' accomplishments, it took some time to realize what a remarkable life Howard Thompson has led.

Thompson was born and raised in the Spruce View district and now lives on land purchased from the Hudson's Bay in 1917 by his Norwegian parents, who came to the area in 1902. He's been a family man, farmer, logger, businessman, headmaster, missionary, politician, RCMP, foreign diplomat in Washington D.C. and very busy community volunteer. Wow! Where does one start to describe a life like that?

Unfortunately, in one short column, we can only scratch the surface, so let's begin in 1946 when Thompson and his wife, Olive, decided to take their infant son to Ethiopia. Thompson's elder brother, Bob Thompson (a future M P), was teaching in Ethiopia at the time, so the family were somewhat familiar with conditions in Africa.

Because Thompson was taking farm machinery to Ethiopia, the family traveled by freighter. After 17 days at sea, they took a train to Egypt where they encountered a major problem: baby Ted was too young to receive a yellow fever vaccination, so mother and baby were placed in quarantine by the Egyptian authorities. Despite

Thompson's pleas, the parents and baby were held hostage for days, until a sympathetic TWA airline-owner heard of the young family's plight, cut through the red tape, and flew them to their new home in Jimma, Ethiopia.

Once in Jimma, the Thompsons were amazed to find themselves living in luxurious condos specially constructed for Mussolini's top military men. These military quarters had been vacated the previous spring when South African and British forces drove Mussolini out of Africa. Imagine the thrill of unlocking doors to lavish suites furnished with the finest Italian imports.

"We left three rooms and a path in Alberta to live in a mansion in Africa," Thompson jokes.

The Thompson family home in Jimma

Later, the family wandered around the fifty-acre compound, admiring exotic flowers, banana trees and seeing oxen plowing fertile volcanic soil, the color of sun-dried bricks. Being close to the equator, gardens were planted continuously to ensure an abundance of fresh fruit and vegetables were on the table year-round.

Thompson's assignment was to convert the deserted military base into a trade school. He quickly set about redesigning buildings, developing a curriculum and hiring staff. Employed by the Ethiopian Board of Education operating under Emperor Haile Selassie, Thompson's official job description was "Headmaster," and Olive's was "Secretary."

Thompson had not worked on such an enormous task before, especially in the field of education, so he enlisted Miss Elsa Gundesen, a retired teacher from Dickson, Alberta, to head the teacher-training program. Assisted by Miss Gundesen and Finley Barnes, Superintendent of Schools from Rocky Mountain House, Thompson developed a school's curriculum, styled after the Olds College program of studies. School opened with 120 male students enrolled in general education, animal husbandry, carpentry, motor mechanics and first aid.

The Practical Arts School was a huge success—so much so that when Howard met Emperor Selassie later that year, the emperor said, "I want to put on a banquet at your agricultural school, and I want to go (as an observer) into every classroom."

Photo taken in 1948 at Ambo Agricultural College. Howard on Haile Salassie's left, and Olive and small son, Ted, are on Salassie's immediate right.

True to his word, the Emperor arrived the following Monday, accompanied by his beloved dogs. Then came a sumptuous banquet befitting a great benevolent ruler—which Selassie was. Thompson recalls the Emperor as "a good, Christian man whose fondest dream was to educate his people."

Howard Thompson sits in the midst of his students after their team won a fast ball game in Addis Ababa (1948)

In the years the Thompson family lived in Jimma, they made many friends and had many exciting adventures. "Those were the most unforgettable years of my life," Thompson says.

Following a three-year term at the Agricultural School, Thompson was appointed educational attaché, and in 1949 he was transferred to the Ethiopian Embassy in Washington D.C. In this position he travelled thousands of miles administering finances, tuition and living allowances for Ethiopian students enrolled in universities in the states and Canada.

When Thompson and family returned to Spruce View, they brought with them a very special young man, Kassa Wolde Mariam, whom they regarded as their adopted son. While here, Wolde Mariam attended community events, pitched in with farm chores and for two years attended Three Hills Prairie Bible Institute. Later, Wolde Mariam attended Seattle Pacific College where he obtained his Master's degree.

Kassa Wolde Mariam (right) sits proudly atop a round corral he helped build on Thompson's Spruce View farm.

On his return to Ethiopia, the Thompsons were elated to receive word of Wolde Mariam's marriage to Emperor Haile Selassie's granddaughter. Who could predict this happy event would have such tragic consequences?

Thompson still recalls the horror of 1974 when he learned a military coup had seized power in Ethiopia. During the uprising, the 83 year-old emperor was murdered—suffocated in the basement of the Imperial Palace on August 27, 1975. Cited as a direct descendant of King Solomon and the Queen of Sheba, Emperor Haile Selassie had ruled Ethiopia for 44 years. During his reign, Selassie was responsible for translating the New Testament to Amharic for his people and made great strides in educating the masses. He was also the last emperor in a dynasty that stretched over one thousand years.

To ensure the end of this ancient kingdom, the Russian military rounded up anyone with connections to the Royal Family. Consequently, Kassa Wolde Mariam faced a firing squad with other royal members on New Year's Day, 1976, and was shot and buried in a mass grave.

Living among the people of Ethiopia has left Thompson with many memories, some happy and some indescribably sad. His fondest memories are of Salassie, a great Ethiopia Emperor, who drew on Central Alberta expertise to bring education to African youth and Kassa Wolde Mariam, the young Ethiopian who endeared himself to all he met in Alberta.

Three years ago Thompson made a return visit to Jimma and was pleased to discover the Practical Arts School he opened in 1945 has grown into a huge, fully accredited university. Named Jimma University, it is one of the largest in the country. Another pleasant surprise was the hero's welcome he received. The staff treated him royally and gave him a two-day tour of the campus.

"Two of Mussolini's sixty-year-old duplexes are still in use," Thompson says, "and the educational complex originally commissioned by King Solomon's descendant is (by coincidence or divine providence) currently governed by a president named Solomon.

To learn more about Howard's eventful life, read his soon-to-be released book of memoirs.

A guaranteed page-turner, the new book includes humorous accounts of Howard as a young RCMP constable hunting for fugitives. It also features the rousing camaraderie of the RCMP Centennial Ride of 1999, when Howard, age 80, completed over 100 km on horseback during a three-day camp-out from Red Deer to the historic fort at Rocky Mountain House.

Hats off to a life well lived!

Local library more that 100 years old

The Idunn Library, located in a cluster of farm buildings near Markerville, is thought to be the oldest standing library in Alberta.

It's hard to believe the little building is more than 100 years old. From the outside, it certainly doesn't look that old.

New cedar shingles and a fresh coat of paint has given the exterior a contemporary look, but step inside and you find yourself in a time capsule—back in the horse and buggy days.

Everything's original, from the beautiful unpainted, spruce walls to the book shelves that span the width of the building.

A counter with a hinged entry separates the bookshelves from the reading area and benches, built decades ago, grace the left wall.

There's also a certain ambiance about the place that makes it easy to imagine the tromping of boots entering the library or a reader choosing a book before hunkering down beside the airtight heater to enjoy prose or poetry written in the Icelandic language.

Many of the library's 583 books were collected as early as 1891 through the efforts of Jonas Hunford, Johann Bjornson and Einar B. Oddson.

A year later the library was officially opened and named "Idunn" after the mythological goddess of fertility, death and eternal youth.

Since Bjornson had a fairly large house, both the Idunn Library and the Tindastoll Post Office operated from his home.

When the first wave of Icelanders arrived west of Red Deer in 1888, Tindastoll, named for a mountain in Iceland, became the hub of the Icelandic community. The residents were proud of their post office, library, school and cemetery—the only hints of civilization for miles around.

After C.P. Marker, Dairy Commissioner for Alberta, opened a creamery approximately six kilometers west of Tindastoll in 1899, the town of Markerville sprang up around the new industry. Folks soon drifted to the new center, which in turn led to Tindastoll's eventual demise. Following are a few statistics worth remembering about Markerville and the once vibrant community of Tindastoll.

Tindastoll Post Office never moved to Markerville, as commonly believed. Markerville Post Office opened in 1902, according to the Geographic Board of Canada, and closed Feb 12, 1991, whereas the Tindastoll Post Office operated from June 1, 1892 to December 21, 1912.

Tindastoll School opened Feb 3, 1899 and closed in June 1955. School classes began in Markerville in 1902 and ended in 1959.

Tindastoll Cemetery is still a place of solitude and beauty, however the first settlers interred there fell victim to a flood and had to be exhumed and laid to rest on higher ground.

As for Tindastoll's library, when lots were surveyed in Markerville in 1903, the Idunn Library Society felt readers would be better served in the new town.

In 1907 the society purchased a town lot and erected the library building which remains standing after 101 useful years.

Idunn Library Society had twenty-three charter members, and membership dues were fifty cents annually. All of the books were printed in Icelandic. Idunn Library was opened Mondays, and Jonas Hunford took on the job as volunteer librarian.

He loved working in the library even though it meant a daily six-mile (10 km) walk. Eventually his health failed, and his son, Harry, took over as librarian until he, too, passed away. The last librarian was Jon Christvinnson who resided in the hamlet.

As time went on, the Icelanders learned English and attendance declined.

Finally, the Idunn Library closed and the books were given away.

In 1955, when the late Mrs. Leslie Johnston realized the library was abandoned, she asked custodian, Jon Christvinnson, if the society would consider selling the building.

"How much do you want for it?" she asked.

"One hundred dollars," Christvinnson replied. Although a hundred dollars was a lot of money in those days, the Johnstons bought the little library and moved it to its present site on Valley Crest Farm, 4 kilometers north of Markerville.

Appreciating the library's historic significance, Johnstons have always kept the building in good repair. In 2007, grandson Leslie repainted, shingled and straightened the walls to give the little library a new lease on life.

The restoration of Idunn Library is only one of the many projects Leslie Johnston has undertaken to preserve local history. In 2005, Johnston built an entire model community.

This included a model village of Markerville, Stephansson House and Hola School with respective outbuildings and proportionate figurines—all to scale and all as they appeared in the early 1900s. These model buildings are displayed on special occasions on the lawn of the Historic Markerville Creamery Museum which opens for the tourist season mid-May each year.

Valley Crest Farm, home of Idunn Library, is an historic entity in itself, having been owned by the Johnston family since 1903.

Idunn Library is shown by appointment only. To book a visit call Les at 403-318-2566 or 403-728-3566

Classic old barn still standing

Have you ever driven the QE2 and noticed the "Gee Road" sign west of Ponoka, then glanced to the east and seen an impressive old barn perched on a hill near a grove of spruce trees?

If this is the case, then you'll be interested in the history of this particular farmstead and the folks who once owned the land.

Walter L. Gee, pioneer landowner, arrived in the area from Missouri around 1910 and, having fallen heir to a considerable sum of money, set up one of the most successful business and agricultural operations in western Canada.

Gee had a special interest in heavy horses (there were no farm tractors in the area at the time), so he purchased registered Clydesdale breeding stock and set about farming his 2,100 acres of land.

Since well bred horses require extra care, a huge barn was built—the same barn seen by travellers of the QE2, today.

My father, William Lees, who arrived in the country in 1912, hired on to help build the barn in 1914.

Dad was fearless when it came to heights. To quote him, "the taller the building, the better the view," so swinging from rafters while roofing Gee's barn was considered 'fun' for the English teenager.

A new immigrant without parents in Canada, the eighteen-year-old appreciated both the employment and the kindness shown him by Gee, his wife and young son, Merle.

Father remembered Walter Gee as being a fair-minded man; his wife as being very motherly as well as an exceptional cook, and Merle, then not much more than a toddler, seated on a milking stool, combing the fetlocks of a very patient Clydesdale.

Barn construction began in 1913, and the bottom portion of the walls were cement which had to be mixed

William Lees on the top rafter while building the barn

and poured by hand.

When finished, the cement walls were almost a meter thick. In fact they were so strong it took several weeks to chop a doorway through a wall when a milking parlour was added a few years later.

An interesting facet of the 80 by 40 foot barn was a one-story hayloft which butted into the hillside. The incline of the hill, coupled with the height of the building, allowed horse-drawn hayracks to be driven into the loft, thus alleviating the arduous task of forking the hay up into the loft.

Originally, the barn held stalls for 12 teams of massive workhorses as well as box stalls for registered Clydesdales stallions, brood mares and foals.

In 1919, after the barn was fully completed, the Gee family built a 1,600 sq. foot home.

Luxurious in its day, the frame house featured a spacious parlor with rock fireplace, kitchen and dining room on the main floor. A wide carpeted stairway with beveled stair rails led to four large bedrooms on the second floor.

In later years, Walter and son, Merle, opened a gravel pit on the southern portion of the land and worked the pit with the family-owned mining equipment: crushers, back hoes and a fleet of gravel trucks. This endeavor also met with success.

Following his father's death, Merle took charge of the family business until his own sudden death in 1988. However, history lives on. Descendants of these early pioneers still retain all 2,100 acres of the original property, and family members continue to live on the farmstead as keepers of the land.

Gee's barn today can be seen from the QE2 Highway

Pictured above is Dick Hollingsworth, rodeo organizer and fine western gentleman. Below, his son Artie pleases rodeo fans with the famous Hollingsworth bronc-ride.

Hollingsworth family known for rodeos

Melissa Hollingsworth, Central Alberta's own Olympic medallist, has just returned home from an African tour.

Along with three other high profile athletes, Hollingsworth visited Guana from April 6-11, 2009 as a Canadian ambassador with an organization named "Right to Play."

The sole purpose of the athletes' visit was to encourage African youngsters to participate in sports—to let them know it's okay to play games, compete and have fun.

Although she enjoyed her trip, Hollingsworth had to admit it was highly disturbing to see civil war victims in refugee camps.

"We saw how raw conditions were and how vulnerable children are," she said. "Yet, knowing we made a difference was rewarding."

Canadians, particularly Albertans, can be duly proud of how well this young lady is representing us on the world stage.

Hollingsworth won a bronze medal at the Olympics in Turin, Italy, in 2006 for skillfully maneuvering her sled around curves at speeds exceeding 120 km. per hour, and she plans to compete in 2010 in Vancouver's winter Olympics.

She also participated last month in the 2008 World Championship Skeleton Races in Altenberg, Germany.

The Hollingsworth families—six generations of them—are best known in Alberta for their century-long involvement in rodeo, and have a solid reputation for being fearless in competition and, more importantly, cheerful losers as well as humble winners.

Melissa's great-great grandfather, Robert Lee Hollingsworth (Dick) was born in California in 1869 and came to Alberta in 1902.

He was a quiet-spoken man with lively brown eyes and a white goatee.

It was a regular sight to see him in black western attire, riding his long-legged, bay gelding past Aurora, the one-room school his grandsons, Gilbert, Earl and Lee, attended.

Grandpa Hollingsworth, as we neighbour kids respectfully called him, was a true gentleman in every sense of the word.

Agile as a cat, he was still climbing yard light poles to replace bulbs in his 80s and riding fast-paced horses well into his 90s. Here lies the secret behind Melissa's athletic ability—genetics.

Grandpa Hollingsworth, along with sons, Stanley and Artie, used to hold Sunday rodeos in the late 1930s and early '40s at their home on the Moose Horn Ranch west of Leedale.

Old-fashioned, stampedes, they were, too, the real wild-west kind old-timers brag about.

There was lots of hair-raising action at these affairs, followed by dances with local musicians playing fiddles, guitars, banjos and mouth harps.

At age four, I attended my first Hollingsworth rodeo, not on the Moose Horn Ranch, mind you, but on the NE 27-41-5-W5, north of Leslieville. This land belonged to Ray McBride at the time, but many owners later, it became the Olympic medallist's childhood home when her father, Darcy Hollingsworth, purchased it.

This first rodeo ingrained itself in my memory because an angry black bull cleared a pole fence and scared the living daylights out of me. Years after the incident, I was visiting the late Artie Hollingsworth, Melissa's great uncle.

He recalled watching in horror as the bull charged toward me.

"I put Jack Elliot on that bull," Artie remembered. "My dad, Dick, was announcing the event on a bullhorn, and we were all pretty tense when the bull headed toward this little kid. As luck would have it, the bull had his mind set on a distant pasture and no one was hurt."

Artie laughed when I told him I still dreamt of black bulls. Then he related a nightmare of his own which happened in July 1925 in the Leedale Valley.

Artie was eleven at the time, helping his father in the hayfields. Dick had previously warned young Artie never to fool with horses in the vicinity of the hay camp. Nevertheless, when a horse named Laddie came galloping past the tents, Artie couldn't resist the temptation. Mounted on his saddle pony, Artie tossed his lariat and as the rope settled over the intruder's head, it started bucking.

The eleven year-old had taken a couple of dallies around his saddle horn—not a good move—for when the slack came out of the rope, Laddie reared and fell backward into one of the tents. Unfortunately, the tent belonged to Artie's father who was preparing a meal for the haying crew over an open fire. The tent was on one side of the fire pit, a muddy little creek on the other. Looking up from his cooking pot, the senior Hollingsworth was more than a little surprised to see a horse thrashing about on his neatly made bed.

That was bad enough, but as the horse scrambled to his feet, the folding cot clamped onto its back like a giant mouse trap. Poor Laddie! He was terrified and started running—blindly, of course—because the canvas tent had been yanked from its stakes, and covered the horse, head to feet.

Attempting to escape the rampaging horse, Artie's father hurled himself backward, and, you guessed it, lost his footings and fell into the creek.

"I can still remember my dad surfacing," Artie told me. "Dad's teeth were still clamped on a corncob pipe that was upside down and spouting water, and his straw hat was floating down the creek. To cap it all off, the sight of a galloping tent, spooked a team raking hay in a nearby field, and the driver got one heck of a ride through the swamp."

Artie grinned as he recalled the rest of the story.

"Let me tell you, there wasn't much left of the hay camp when Laddie got finished with it. So, I put the spurs to my pony and struck out for a neighbour's place and didn't come home 'til Dad regained his sense of humor."

Regardless of the circumstances, it seems the Hollingsworths' high spirits and sense of humor have always prevailed. Fearless competitors, they continue to defy danger and live life to its fullest.

Melissa has two sports-minded sisters, Laramie and Casidy Hollingsworth, who compete in boxing and barrel racing, respectively. Last year, Laramie won bronze in Championship Boxing, while Casidy placed third out of 150 pole-bending contestants at the World Finals in Gallop, New Mexico.

With the same fortitude and true grit of their ancestors, it's heartening to see new generations of Hollingsworths making history for Canada in the World of Sports.

Stories spring to life at Stephansson House

Stephansson House, the home of Central Alberta's "late-great" poet, Stephan G. Stephansson, is now open for summer visitors.

And what a delightful place to spend a relaxing afternoon! For many years now, the pretty pink cottage, three kilometers north and two west of Markerville, has been a main attraction for travelers from every corner of the globe—each and every one of them anxious to see where the famous poet lived from 1889 until his death in 1927.

Stephansson was born in 1853 and, although he

emigrated from Iceland at the age of twenty and spoke fluent English, he continued to write in Icelandic. This made it difficult, if not impossible, for Albertans to appreciate the poet's genius while he lived among them. However, in recent years Stephansson's work has been translated into English and—posthumously—the poet is being recognized by Canadians as an extremely gifted craftsman. Named *The Poet of The Rocky Mountains*, Stephansson was a self-educated man whose writings possess a distinctive earthy tone punctuated by sensitivity and compassion.

On visiting Stephansson House Provincial Park for the first time, guests are often taken aback by the "pink" bungalow. Attractive as the lovely magenta walls are, the colour still tends to raise eyebrows. Was the house originally pink?

Old-timers believe pioneer families were far too frugal to paint their homes pink. However, many of the early settlers did paint their walls—inside and out—with whitewash. The main ingredient of this creamy paint substitute was excavated from white calcareous mud pits in the area and often acquired a pinkish hue with age.

Some of Stephansson's descendants claim their grandparents' house was never pink, but "a creamy beige" before its restoration in 1982.

In an article to the Icelandic newspaper, *Lögberg-Heimskringla* (June, 2006), Stephansson's granddaughter, Iris Bourne, explained that around 1945, she and her friend, Esther Finsson, tried their hand at redecorating.

"We decided to paint the bedroom which used to be my grandmother's bedroom and get it freshened up because the girls were sleeping there," she remembered. "So, we kind of decided on pink. So, Esther's mother got the pink kalsomine, which was the main paint ingredient in those days—you mix so much water in the kalsomine—and we painted it (the bedroom) all nice, and we bought a little can of enamel to do the windowsills and door facings.

"Of course, when we went to clean our brushes, where did we clean them? We went around to the back side of the house (and) cleaned the brushes by wiping them on the wall." Iris then goes on to say Provincial historians found pink paint chips on the exterior wall and, insisted on painting the whole building that colour regardless of protests from the family.

In spite of the existing controversy over the pretty pink exterior, the interior of the house is delightfully original. And should visitors let their mind wander, they can visualize a studious poet sitting in his swivel chair, pen in hand and elbow resting on his desk, writing eloquent verses, while Helga, his wife, putters in the kitchen.

Similar to many pioneer women, Helga was the main stay of the family. Since her husband was engrossed in his writing, Helga kept the farm going. Besides her daily farm and household chores, she grew a large vegetable garden and raised her own sheep.

After sheering the sheep, she took the fleeces to the river, waded in and washed the wool in the running water. After that, she carded and spun the wool before knitting it into saleable articles to supplement the farm income. When her husband traveled on speaking engagements to the States, Iceland and Europe, Helga usually remained at home, caring for her children, the farm and an elderly mother-in-law.

It's evident Stephansson admired his wife when he wrote, "Her smile in particular was all that triumph depended on, that kept everything afloat."

A few of Stephansson's romantic lyrics, written when he was courting Helga, still exist today, leading readers to believe theirs could be rated as one of Alberta's most poignant love stories.

Similar to Stephan, Helga was born in Iceland, and according to her father, Jón Jónsson, life in Iceland had become so traumatic by 1873, the family were forced to emigrate. Jónsson's diary entry for January of that year reads, "Blizzards and heavy snowfalls (occurred) from thorri through the twelfth week of winter, consequently no pasture. Both the ground and snow are frozen hard. On the tenth, the fall of volcanic ash was so heavy the snow turned dark reddish brown to the depth of about an inch. On some farms (volcanic) explosions are heard and in the southwest flames can be seen."

Helga

Helga was fourteen when she travelled with her parents and younger brother, Jón, to America—a party of four, as her father related, with very little money.

"We found shelter and work with Norwegian farmers in Wisconsin," Jónsson said, "and wages were paid in flour, potatoes, bacon and meat."

Even young Helga was sent to work as a farm labourer and, in 1874, Jonsson announced proudly, "Little Helga earned almost thirty dollars in our first year in America and little Jón earned ten…and my total earnings over the year were one hundred and twenty dollars."

With money in his pocket, Jónsson purchased 80 acres of land for $39, constructed a building "that passes for a house," cleared two acres of land, purchased two cows and five ewes as well as garden seed.

Yet, Jónsson's high hopes came to nothing. On August 1875, he announced bitterly that he'd cut his foot with a scythe and couldn't work, a ewe died, his cows produced very little milk and his garden was extremely poor due to dry weather and cabbage worms.

"The money is gone and food supplies are already in short supply. We have taken up and eaten almost five bushels of potatoes, which apart from milk and a little bread, we are now living on exclusively."

In April 1876, Jónsson reported that Helga was working for Americans. This was a blessing because he'd suffered another accident, this time accidentally cutting his knee.

"I've been confined to my bed all month, one of the most tedious periods of my life, and God knows I have had little enjoyment or pleasure from life since moving from my own home and that of my fathers."

However, other countrymen lived in the vicinity. One young Icelander was Stephan G. Stephansson who not only formed a partnership in a logging operation with Jonsson in 1877, but presented Helga with romantic verses composed especially for her.

A year later on August 26, 1878, Stephan married Helga, and in due time the couple had eight children, of which only six lived to adulthood. After parting company with Helga's parents and brother in North Dakota, Stephansson moved his family to Central Alberta in

1889, and the rest is history best told on location.

Certainly, there are many more stories—some happy, some sad—but all guaranteed to come alive when you visit Stephansson House this summer. For on site information phone 403-728-3929.

Helga Stephansson, wife of a famous Icelandic poet.

A pint-sized Markerville community

Leslie Johnston would never think of himself as a history teacher, and he's not a fellow to knuckle down over a history book.

Yet, make no mistake, Johnston has devised some unique ways to tell the history of his community to people of all ages.

As a Centennial project, in 2005, Johnston began constructing model buildings representing the district of Hola and Markerville.

Initially, he researched old photographs, converting to scale the measurements of doors, windows and the shape of buildings before he began the actual construction. Then Johnston built exact replicas of schools, churches, residents and businesses as they appeared near his grandparents' farm in 1905.

Each buildings is about the size of an old fashioned doll house. There are twenty-four buildings in all, not counting numerous outdoor biffies.

Among the buildings is Hola School where tiny porcelain children play on swings and teeter-totters. There's Stephansson House painted pink, of course, and decorated with trellises full of ivy.

Beside various residences, there are two churches, a community hall, a rustic creamery complete with cream cans, a pool hall, butcher shop, library, Benediktson's and Johnson's stores with small tools and barrels of apples in shop windows.

Real hay spills out of the loft of Morkeberg's old red barn, and laundry flaps in the breeze on a clothesline outside the Markerville Hotel.

June is the month when school students tour the Historic Markerville Creamery, so it's gratifying to watch children hop off school busses and make a bee-line for the model community.

Some of the younger students immediately slide to a stop, belly down and peer into tiny windows, then open miniature hinged doors and let their imaginations take them back to the days of their great-grandparents.

For hundreds of visitors, young and not-so-young, this "hands-on" display presents history in a most enjoyable and meaningful way.

For the past three years, these diminutive buildings and their entourage of little people have ridden on floats, sat on the front lawn of the Red Deer County Administration Building and traveled to Hola School and Stephansson House for special functions. Until Canada Day this year, the models can be viewed on the lawn of Historic Markerville Creamery.

Many other exhibits pertaining to Markerville Museum have been improved by Johnston's touch of ingenuity. He's added imitation butter to museum platens, authentic looking coals to fire the creamery boiler and created effigies of former employees to direct visitors to parking areas. Johnston is also a skilled cartoonist, bringing history to life in humorous sketches. As well, he and his friends manufactured a cream-can ride to provide free tours of the historic town of Markerville.

Recently, Johnston restored the Idunn Library, which housed Icelandic library books collected as early as 1889. For preserving this historic building, Johnston and his family, received the 2008 Heritage Recognition Award from the Red Deer and District Museum Society at a special ceremony on May 26 in Red Deer County Council Chambers.

Vera, Les and Kelly Johnston accepting the 2008 Heritage Recognition Award

Idunn library is open to visitors and is located on Valley Crest Farm, a farm established by Johnston's grandparents in 1903.

Here, along with younger brother, Kelly, Johnston raises hay, green-feed and a large herd of Gelbvich Shorthorn cattle—that is when he isn't working on another history project.

Similar to Arizona's Baboquivari Peak (shown above), Alberta's Devil's Head Mountain (below), has served as a landmark to guide travellers for countless centuries.

Devil's Head Mountain has its share of weirdness

There is a mountain in southern Arizona that claims a lot of attention from vacationers since its great rocky cliffs can be seen for a hundred miles in any direction.

Rising up 2357 meters from the dessert floor, Baboquivari Peak speaks of romance, tragedy and ancient history.

Not unlike other unique edifices, Baboquivari is steeped in legend. With its huge granite face, it has been credited with human characteristics, smiling on some visitors while eating others alive.

To this day, the native Tohonto O'odham believe the flat-faced precipice is the home of the creator, I'otoi, who resides in a cave below the mountain and watches over the O'odham people.

Watchful?

Perhaps.

Protective?

No, for its sprawling slopes have been bathed in the blood of hundreds of warring natives and ambushed travelers.

From 1540 through the 1800s, Spanish Conquistadors, Franciscan and Jesuit priests, cattle drovers, miners and stage drivers found their way through the desert by taking their bearings from the mountain's distinctive

Devil's Head Mountain in the Rocky Mountain Range can be seen throughout Central Alberta.

Below (right) is a view of **Devil's Head Mountain** as seen from Geniffer Lake—Dickson Damn

features. Some passed in safety; others did not.

Many Central Albertans would be surprised to learn we have a mountain remarkably similar in appearance to Baboquivari with corresponding tales of triumph and disaster.

Named Devil's Head by the Stoney people, our own flat-face peak is every bit as captivating as its Arizona counterpart. At 2997 meters, Devil's Head is slightly taller than Baboquivari, lies on the eastern front of the Rockies and can be seen for a hundred miles or more by those living (or traveling) in the corridor between Red Deer and Calgary.

The Devil's Head is easiest to identify in winter when its vertical cliffs shed snow and remain dark in contrast to the white caps of the surrounding mountains.

Not surprisingly, early travelers used this curious looking peak as a landmark by which to plot their route through Central Alberta. Explorer Peter Fidler was the first white man to mention the peak by name.

A journal entry, dated 1792, states Fidler took his bearings on, "a remarkably high cliff of the Rocky Mountains called by our people (the Stoney people traveling with him), the Devil's Head."

In 1841 George Simpson also mentioned the peak when his party passed Devil's Head, saying, "It has a rude resemblance to an upturned face."

Again, on August 7, 1858, James Hector wrote, "Half an hour after starting this morning we came to Deadman's River and found that the plain we had been admiring the previous evening was really the valley which rises near the Devil's Head."

Similar to its southern cousin, Baboquivari Peak, the Devil's Head has its share of spine-tingling tales. The Cree were reported to be so fearful of the peak, they left conciliatory offerings of pipes, tobacco and decorated tomahawks on its rock ledges.

There are also accounts of fierce battles being fought between Blackfoot and Kootenai people in nearby Devil's Gap. During these skirmishes, many tribesmen were killed, and legend has it that a ghost can be seen in the evenings drifting up and down the Ghost River, gathering the skulls of slain warriors.

The same legend is said to be responsible for naming other entities in the vicinity of Devil's Head, such as Apparition Peak, Phantom Crag and the Ghost River (previously named Deadman's River).

To see Devil's Head at close range, take the Forestry trunk road (#940) to the Ghost River Road, follow this for 15.6 kilometers to a campground and enjoy the view over a picnic lunch.

For those with lots of stamina and a stout pair of boots, there's also a relatively good hiking trail leading from the campground up an old telephone cut-line to Black Rock Mountain Lookout.

The trail is steep, so allow nine hours for this 18 km hike, then be prepared for a breathtaking view of Devil's Head and the Ghost River region.

With the high price of fuel, more Central Albertans are opting to travel shorter distances. Come to think of it, traveling Alberta does make "cents." Why visit mountains in far away places when we have our own five-star attractions right here at home?

Intriguing stories behind Indian Flats

This year wild roses and blue bells are plentiful along country roads, and their fragrance brings back memories of Sundances held, long ago, in the vicinity of Lampman Valley west of Rimbey.

Why several hundred people of the First Nation chose this location for their annual religious ceremonies between 1935 and 1945 is unknown, but come they did, from all parts of Alberta and Saskatchewan. They began arriving in mid June.

Those coming from the east crossed the Medicine River at Leedale and continued west past Aurora School, then veered northwest on a bush trail to their camp-grounds on Indian Flats.

Others traveled various dirt roads from south and west of Leslieville, before taking the same cut-off north of Block's Creek.

Each summer for the ten consecutive years, children attending Aurora's old log school on the hill watched long processions of horses, wagons, kids and dogs, stretching as far as the eye could see in every direction.

Most of the neighbours attended the Sundances as spectators. In those days, everyone traveled by saddle horse or team and wagon, so the sound of voices and creaking, metal-rimmed, wooden wheels made for a great deal of noise as lumber wagons bumped along the rutted trail to the SE 8-42-R5-W5, then a Hudson's Bay quarter.

My most vivid recollection was that of approaching the ceremonial site and seeing a group of women and children.

One young woman, not more than fifteen or sixteen, had a baby strapped to her back. A hatchet was in her hand, and she was stripping bark from a tree and eating it, while the toddler tugging at her skirt, sucked on a gopher tail.

Indian Flats, as they were called, consisted of grassy meadows bordered by poplar, spruce and pine. A small creek ran along the edge of the largest meadow (about 30 acres). Shortly after the travellers arrived, the outer edge of this meadow was dotted with white canvas tents erected by the womenfolk.

In the center of this large meadow, a ceremonial lodge was built. First, a massive central pole was raised. This was ringed by smaller poles to form a circle approximately twelve meters in diameter.

Next the outer portion of the structure was walled with leafy poplar branches.

Bolts of brightly coloured fabric were hung from the central pole and, on the inside of the lodge, a curved partition approximately a meter high, was constructed by weaving willows together.

When all was complete, elders built a small fire in the center of the lodge to heat a pan of ceremonial offerings, and dancers took up positions behind the willow partition. Then with the beating of drums, dancing commenced—females on one side of the lodge, males on the other. Outside, young braves chanted as they circled the lodge on horseback. The purpose of this religious ceremony was to praise and petition the Maker for special blessings. All participants fasted, and some danced seventy-two hours with only short breaks between dances.

Such a large gathering of people required a huge amount of food, so local farmers were quick to capitalize on the event by selling eggs, milk, home baking and garden vegetables to the first nation people. Needless to say, the whole community welcomed the native buyers, for these were depression days and regular farm incomes were non-existent.

Perhaps the happiest salesperson was Florry Robb who owned a home-based store in the area. Not only did the Cree purchase food en route to their campground, but Robb packed tea, coffee, sugar, flour and whatever else her wagon would carry to Indian Flats where she set up a mobile shopping center.

Yet not all entrepreneurs met with success, as a young man by the name of Bill discovered. The following anecdote told to me by the budding salesman, himself, was later recorded in *Hoofprints to Highways—Leslieville and Districts History Book.*

Bill's adventure (or misadventure; had it not been for good luck and a fast horse he may never have lived to tell about it) began when two young braves asked him to bring some liquid refreshments to the annual gathering at Indian Flats. Thinking the idea had merit, Bill borrowed a dozen quart sealers, filled them full of moonshine and set off to make his fortune. Arriving at the camp, the young peddler was invited into a tent where a gambling game was in full swing. However, after dipping into the moonshine the gamblers grew loud and quarrelsome. At the height of the commotion, an older tribesmen barged into the tent.

"What's going on in here?" he yelled, and his eyes filled with hate when he spotted the hooch and the white man responsible for bringing it.

Snatching up the bottles, Bill crammed them into a gunny sack and ran for his horse. Then, throwing himself into the saddle, he set off at a gallop. "It wasn't long before I heard them coming," Bill said. "With their ki-yi's and war whoops, they were hot on my trail."

Knowing he couldn't outrun twenty-five or thirty native riders, Bill hid in the bushes, his heart pounding in his chest as he waited for his pursuers to pass by. Luckily, they did, and as the thunder of hooves died away, Bill set off in the opposite direction. After riding hard all night, he reached home territory at daybreak. However, all but one of the glass jars he'd promised to return were broken.

The following day two very sober young Cree came to see if he was still in one piece. "You made it home all right?" One of them asked. "Didn't catch you?"

"No, they didn't catch me," Bill said. "What would they have done if they had caught me?"

"I dunno—maybe kill you."

At the time Bill had seen a number of Westerns at the theatre, so in the dark of night the prospect of being scalped alive seemed very real. Scary? Perhaps!

Yet others recall roses and bluebells blooming along the trail to Indian Flats and folks of both races visiting in harmony—pleasant memories of a colourful annual pilgrimage which came to a grinding halt when, for some unknown reason, the Hudson's Bay sold the ceremonial grounds and uprooted a fine tradition.

Mounties surprise bad guys to make arrest

Sketch by Melissa Gray-Barry

Outlaws were few and far between in the Rocky Mountain House area in 1907.

For one thing, there weren't many people near Mountain House—as the settlement was then called—and most could be described as God fearing folk.

I suspect the next two stories about an outlaw may have described the same incident from different perspectives.

The first is taken from the *Mountaineer's Old Timer's Series*; the second was told by an early resident, Ira Gray.

First, from the *Mountaineer*:

"It was about 1907 that a horse thief by the name of King, holed up on the west side of the North Saskatchewan River, near the present town.

Two Mounties had been on his trail for two days. Then began a cat and mouse game. When the Mounties crossed the river, King would hide. After several attempts to nab him without success, the two Mounties went back and camped on the east side of the river.

"Sergeant Nickelson who would later become an Inspector, decided he had had enough with the shenanigans, so keeping out of sight, Nickelson under cover, left the other Mountie on the river bank and went two miles downstream. Nickelson then took off his clothes, tied them on his back, and swam to the west side.

"While the horse thief was intently watching the Mountie camp on the other side, Nickelson came up from behind and, much to King's surprise he was placed under arrest."

From Ira Gray's memoirs comes this story: In 1907, Ira's father, Tom, was moving the family from Medicine Lodge Hills (now, Sunset Hills), west of Bentley, to his newly acquired property (SE 13-39-8-W5), west of the North Saskatchewan River.

Tom, never did anything by halves, so besides his wife and four sons, he had a great entourage of wagons, machinery, cattle and horses, all of which he'd brought from the Dakotas the previous year. It was slow going, especially while herding livestock, so the family camped several times along the way.

One night a stranger rode into camp, leading a pack horse. He said his name was Charlie Rider. He was going back to "Mountain House," and wanted to ride along with the Gray party.

Tom was immediately suspicious. "Why does this fellow want to accompany a slow moving procession, when a man on horseback can make much better time, alone?" he wondered.

The more Tom mulled the question over in his mind, the more uneasy he began to feel. "Watch out for that fellow," Tom cautioned his family. "He's a strange one!"

When Grays arrived at the North Saskatchewan River, there were no bridges, so they needed to ford the river below present day Highway 11A bridge.

The old trail was steep, narrow and made a sharp left-hand turn just before it crossed Stump Creek and dropped down to the river.

Ira, then 13, was driving a buggy carrying his mother and baby brother. Access to the river lay through a heavily wooded ravine, and as Ira drove his team around the bend in the trail, he saw a tent set up in front of the creek and a man squatting beside it. Tents and campers were common sights, so Ira thought nothing of it.

At the time, the tag-along stranger was riding directly in front of Ira's buggy. They reached the creek and started into the water, when the man by the fire jumped to his feet. There was a pistol in his hand, and he ordered Charlie Rider to put his hands in the air. As it turned out the gunman was a Mountie in plainclothes, and the tag-along was a wanted man.

Charlie Rider—or whoever the rider was—had obviously been surprised. For that matter, everyone was surprised, including the Mountie who seemed ill prepared to deal with the situation.

Wagons and horses came to an abrupt halt. Ira's team, still on a downhill slope, struggled to keep right-side-up, and other horses could be heard scrambling on the hill behind them. This brought Ira's father to the fore, demanding to know what was holding up the procession. On seeing the stranger with his hands in the air, the elder Gray let out a disgusted huff.

"Well, I knew you were up to no good!" he snapped.

A second RCMP had just set out in a row boat, intending to buy some hay from Hudson Hunt on the opposite side of the river. (The Hunts were living in a dugout near the abandoned fort at the time). Hearing his partner calling, the second RCMP paddled furiously back. Then, and only then, was the wanted man allowed to dismount, and together the two Mounties, both out-of-uniform, made a formal arrest.

The last the Gray family saw of Charlie Rider, he was sitting on a log, in handcuffs and leg-irons.

Could Rider's real name have been "King?" Quite possibly. At any rate, the outlaw left a lasting impression in the mind of thirteen year-old Ira Gray, who often spoke of the incident, recalling each and every detail of the surprise.

This leads to another question. Was the newspaper article one hundred percent accurate—or was it told by an ambitious young Mountie who "got his man" by chance, rather than the reported heroics which put him in line for a promotion?

Myrtle Raivio "Lady Guide Of The Hills"

On the afternoon I visited Pine Grove Cemetery, a chill west wind cut through my jacket and hurled dry leaves among the headstones.

Yet on that blustery day, the wind had little to do with the way my eyes were watering as I read the words chiseled in the granite slab marking Myrtle Raivio's final resting place, "Lady Guide Of The Hills."

What truth those five words held because not only was Myrtle the first woman guide and outfitter in Alberta, she was every inch a lady.

I recall the many times she came into our mechanic shop to have repairs done on her truck. I can picture her now, the curled-up brim of her western hat shading a pair of bright blue eyes, asking in that undemanding way of hers, "Have the boys got time to look at my truck, today?"

At such times I would gladly leave my book work to visit while her truck was being readied for the rough roads she so often traveled.

Over a cup of coffee she quietly pondered over a wide range of local and international events. And believe me, she spoke intelligently on a wide range of subjects.

She loved the mountains, and for over fifty years "Shorty," as she was called, guided both Canadian and American hunters onto the Rocky slopes during a three months long hunting season (Sept. 1st to Nov. 30th).

Other clients, geologists and sightseers, hired her during the summer.

Regardless of the duration of the trip, a minimum of fifteen to twenty-five head of horses were required for each party of travelers and two guides and a cook accompanied each party.

In the fall of 1955 Myrtle operated fifteen camps simultaneously in the mountains west of Nordegg. All told, she used 103 head of horses and hired a packer and cook for each camp.

Later on, while continuing to guide, she owned and operated a large PMU barn and trap line. At one time she had her own sawmill, cutting and skidding the logs herself.

She also built a trapper's cabin, fourteen feet wide and twenty feet long. This was constructed with timbers, squared on three sides, which she raised with a minimum of assistance.

Yet even as Myrtle competed in male dominated occupations, she retained her femininity. In 1962, she was elected Queen of Central Alberta Light Horse Association.

And what a beautiful queen she made! Friends and neighbours remember her as dignified, always appropriately dressed and never gaudy.

Myrtle also volunteered for causes she believed in. When her brother and mother-in-law were long term patients in the Rocky hospital, she not only visited them regularly but dressed, fed and ran errands and pushed wheelchairs for other convalescents.

She was an excellent seamstress, making beautiful clothing for family and friends. She never used a "store-bought" pattern while sewing, but simply took the recipient's measurements and tailored the garment to fit.

Once, when a group of little girls joined dance

classes, Myrtle made each a pretty made-to-measure dance costume. On another occasion, when a pregnant mother couldn't afford a new dress to attend a wedding, Myrtle saved the day by whipping up a stylish maternity dress.

She also made tack for her horses, crafting leather and nylon into bridles, martingales and halters.

She was born Myrtle Sands in Evarts, Alberta on July 21st, 1914. Shortly after birth, she moved with her parents, two brothers and a sister to a remote log cabin on the Baptiste River, 45 miles north-west of Rocky Mountain House. Her father, Clarence Sands, originally trapped for a living. Then, in 1919, he began guiding big game hunters into the mountains.

Living so far from civilization had its drawbacks, but the young Sands family was resourceful, producing their own food, clothing and tack for their horses. Roads were non-existent resulting in tragedy when Myrtle's was four years old and her mother died of appendicitis on route to hospital.

Perhaps it was her mother's untimely death which forced young Myrtle to be ingenious, learning to hunt, fish and trap at an early age. Her first trap lines were rabbit snares set among willows besides their cabin. These she tended daily, knowing how important each pelt was to the welfare of her family.

When her father remarried, Myrtle became a mentor to five more siblings and, after some formal schooling in Slocan City, B. C., she cooked in the camps her father set up for hunters. In 1932 she married Niilo Raivio who predeceased her in 1948. Her two sons, Clarence and Ken Raivio, were her pride and joy.

In 1949, after six years of apprenticeship, Myrtle acquired her own Guide and Outfitters' license, and won many trophies, such as the Rocky Mountain Trophy for registering the largest animals taken each season, during a five year period.

She traveled to Wyoming, Nevada and Louisiana to many annual conventions of the North American Wild Sheep Foundation, set up for the preservation of wild sheep.

These conferences helped Myrtle keep abreast of current big game policies and supplied her with new clients. Here, as well as at functions in Montana, Wisconsin and Hawaii, Myrtle met guides, outfitters, hunters and conservationists from all over the world. Was it any wonder she was able to speak so knowledgeably on international issues?

As a guide and outfitter, Myrtle supplied all the necessities for a well run camp and scheduled the day's activities to suit the needs of her clients. She was known to pay attention to the smallest detail, making sure travelers, both human or equine, were safe, comfortable and well fed.

However, ensuring the safety of others often required Myrtle to put her own life on the line. Son Clarence remembers an incident in 1957 when she narrowly escaped drowning.

Clarence, a teen-ager at the time, was working with his mother guiding a group of geologists in the country south of Chetwynd, British Columbia, and it fell to Myrtle to get her charges safely across two rivers, the Sukunka and the Pine. She assigned the men and supplies to boats, while she, alone, attempted to swim the horses across the Sukunka.

"I told Mom it wouldn't work," Clarence recalls. "It was spring and the Sukunka was running deep and fast, but Mom was determined."

Riding her own stout saddle horse and driving seven horses ahead, Myrtle started into the water. Seconds later, all eight horses were swept away by the raging water.

RAIVIO
MYRTLE LILLIAN
JULY 21, 1914
AUGUST 8, 1982
LADY GUIDE OF THE HILLS

Clarence still shudders as he remembers the horses struggling in the giant whirlpool made by the meeting of the two rivers. After thrashing wildly about, the frenzied animals finally fought their way to shore, but to everyone's horror there was no sign of Myrtle. Presently her body surfaced some distance downstream and a boat went to her rescue.

When pulled from the water she was unconscious, having been struck on the head by the horses' flailing hooves. Yet a day or two later, Myrtle was back in the saddle, directing her crew as if nothing had happened.

Did she enjoy her work? To use Myrtle's own words, she wouldn't trade her life for any other. "Sure it's hard work," she said, "but I just love it."

Myrtle's career was cut short by her death on August 8th, 1982 while she was awaiting heart surgery. Reflecting on her life, Ray Atwater paid her this tribute.

"If you had seen her in that pretty blue serge suit with white hat, shoes and gloves to match, the day she and brother climbed on board the plane to Wisconsin, you would have thought the same as I, that Shorty was indeed the 'Lady Guide of the Foothills.'"

Local historian, a sought-after resource

If you're interested in hearing some intriguing stories from Central Alberta's distant past—say the fur trade, the voyageurs, David Thompson, Father Lacombe or the history of the First Nations—Pat McDonald is the man "in the know."

Pat, a resident of Rocky Mountain House, is well versed in Canadian history, and his popular website, www.davidthompsonthings.com, is proof positive, having logged over 130,000 visitors from 118 countries.

He and his wife, Joan, live a stone's throw from the North Saskatchewan, a river that inspired Pat to write *Where The River Brought Them*. Published in 2000, Pat's book is the official bicentennial history of Rocky Mountain House. The book begins by introducing the famous explorer, David Thompson and his wife, Charlotte Small and takes the reader to present day activities along the North Saskatchewan River.

No doubt about it, Pat McDonald knows his history! That being the case, it can also be said that his own life-story is every bit as interesting as the historical characters he writes about.

Pat grew up near Halifax, Nova Scotia, near Preston and Hammonds Plains, and when he was a lad, these two communities were inhabited predominantly by black Canadians. These people were descendants of the escapees who came to Canada via the underground railway during the American Civil War. So, the black revolution led by Martin Luther King resulted in a good deal of social unrest in Preston, Hammonds Plains and a community called Africaville to the north of Halifax.

"Even in Canada black people were discriminated against," Pat says as he recalls how rudely his black friends were treated on the streets of Halifax.

It seemed Pat had ample opportunity to observe the plight of his coloured neighbours since his father, Tom McDonald, was the foreman of a concrete business comprised mostly of blacks.

"My father quietly, but defiantly, hired only black men because they were good, multi-skilled workers," says Pat, "and concrete for the huge Halifax-Dartmouth bridge was poured mainly by Preston's black workers."

In return for Tom McDonald's kindness, his black employees were fiercely loyal. "They loved my father for believing in them," Pat says, "and, in my younger years, I was by my father's side when he attended black weddings, baptisms and funerals."

Pat's father, a devote Catholic, was a man of principle. With only four years of formal education, he was no stranger to menial, backbreaking labour.

Wanting better for his sons, the senior McDonald insisted his offspring apply themselves to their school studies. This in turn led Pat to earn three University degrees in Art, Education and Law.

It seems these early experiences determined the social issues Pat pursued in later life, such as helping underprivileged children, minority groups and First Nations people.

Lifelong interests have included history, music, literature and sports. In 1986, Pat traveled to China on behalf of the Alberta Government Cultural Exchange Program, coaching clinics for Senior level Chinese basketball coaches.

In 1988 Pat was awarded the Olympic Flame Medal for coaching in Alberta during the Calgary Winter Olympics. In March of this year Pat was inducted into the Shooting Stars Alberta Basketball Coaches Hall of Fame.

After an interesting career in law, Pat, or Mr. Mac as students affectionately called him, served as a Principal of St. Matthew School in Rocky Mountain House.

Since his retirement Pat has written extensively and, besides his full-length book, is the author of several published articles, such as The Metis Settlement of Tail Creek, Maskepatoon–Christian Warriors, Cree Angel and Father Lacombe—The Man of Good Heart.

Pat is a much sought after speaker, making presentations to the Canadian Archaeological Association in Nanaimo, B.C. in 2005 and the Society for American Archaeology in 2008.

In May of this year, Pat spoke to an international audience of Archaeologists and Anthropologists in Rocky Mountain House.

As the main speaker at the Alberta Provincial Boys and Girls High School Basketball Provincial, Pat addressed over 1,000 athletes and guests. He has also presented at a number of historical societies, and this May, Pat was the main speaker at the Alberta Historical Society Annual Banquet—his topic, David Thompson and Charlotte Small.

In 2007, Pat was the recipient of the prestigious award given by the Centennial Alberta Historical Society for promoting history.

He has appeared on the CPAC National Channel and twice has been guest speaker at the Grey Coat School in London, England, the school David Thompson attended.

He was a recent guest on Edmonton's Global TV, presenting the history of Rocky Mountain House. He also appears on Tourism Alberta You Tube with stories of David Thompson.

In 2005, Pat sat on the Repatriation Committee and the Aboriginal Committee to plan the reburials of remains of 26 people who died during the fur trade era, a project which has officially established protocol for future reburials.

As guest speaker for Central Alberta Historical Society in 2009, Pat will be speaking about these reburials on Feb. 19 at 7:30 pm, in the Red Deer Museum.

It's not too early to mark your calendar for this event. Those attending are sure to be intrigued by this great storyteller.

Mr. Churchill added colour to early days

It's a shame so little is known about Horace Churchill.

By all accounts he was a dynamic character who played a unique part in Central Alberta's early history.

He first ventured into Canada sometime between 1903 and 1906, before returning to North Dakota to persuade the Tom Gray family to immigrate to that portion of the North West Territories which later became Central Alberta.

Mr. Churchill (the Gray family always referred to him as mister), was born in the 1840s.

"My mother and father were both killed by Indians," he told the Grays. "Me and my sister escaped by hiding in the bushes and were raised by our grandparents in Illinois."

Between 1861 and '65, Churchill fought in the American Civil War and had the battle scars to prove it. Later, when living in the Dakotas, he owned several hound dogs which earned their keep by hunting coyotes.

The hounds rode in a crate in Churchill's wagon and when turned out, they would search the prairie for the scent of a coyote.

If a coyote was in the vicinity, the dogs would set off at lightning speed, braying loudly, with Churchill lashing his team into a gallop to keep pace.

As they raced across the bumpy prairie, Churchill's long dark hair and beard would be flying in the wind. It was quite a sight!

Although the man had no formal education to speak of, Churchill was a clever carpenter and had worked on various ferry building projects in the Midwest.

A story told about Churchill and his knowledge of ferries concerned the first ferry built at Rocky Mountain House.

Prior to the construction of a railway bridge over the North Saskatchewan River in 1912, the only way to reach Rocky from points west was by fording the river with horses or row boat, a dangerous feat since the Saskatchewan runs swift and deep.

When the Provincial Government sent an engineer from Edmonton to oversee the building of a ferry, there was much celebrating by those living on the west side of the river.

Although Churchill was at the fore, volunteering his expertise, the engineer wanted none of the elderly man's advice. Churchill was said to have been shaking his head in horror as the building was taking place.

"The pylons you're building aren't strong enough to withstand the force of the fast flowing current," he told the engineer, "and your drum and winch apparatus isn't strong enough, either."

The engineers paid no attention to Churchill's warning. After all, what did an old, illiterate hillbilly know?

Then came the day of launching the new ferry—and what a beautiful spring morning it was. The ferry was towed with team and horses down to the river and, with a good deal of pomp and ceremony, the engineer, his crew and scads of local dignitaries pushed off from the banks.

No sooner had the ferry hit the water than the

men aboard felt the strong current propelling the newly built craft across the river. The landing on the west side of the river was quickly made and celebrated with much handshaking and backslapping.

However, on attempting to return to the east bank, when the ferry was angled against the current, the drum mechanism failed.

Next the west pylon toppled over. This let the ferry drift down river until the cable pulled tight which, in turn, pulled the east pylon over. Momentarily, the proud new vessel swooped under the water. Everything loose on deck was washed away, except an axe which someone had struck in the plank flooring.

Had it not been for the newly appointed ferryman grabbing the axe and cutting a rope attached to a cable anchoring the ferry to the fallen pylons, the ferry would surely have sunk.

As it was, the passengers were forced to cling to the ferry railings and ride the bobbing craft down stream until it eventually washed up on a gravel bar, a mile or so away from the actual launch site. The ferry was then tied to a tree and the passengers dripping wet, but thankfully unhurt, walked home.

The next morning a much humbler engineer and his crew took horses down river to retrieve the ferry.

When they got to the place where they'd left the unfortunate vessel, they found the river had risen in the night and both tree and ferry had been washed away.

In the weeks that followed, a new ferry was constructed, this time to Mr. Churchill's satisfaction.

Who was Horace Churchill?

He was a burly, indomitable frontiersman—a likable character who helped to settle the west. Unfortunately, time has erased his actual birth and death date, burial site and much of his activities from the pages of history.

Mr. Churchill and hunting buddies

This photograph was taken near Prairie Grange (the first post office in the Rocky Mountain House area), in 1911 with a camera owned by H. McDonald, the first Presbyterian minister in Rocky. From left to right are folks long deceased: Perry McDermott, Mr. Sponogle, Horace Churchill, Jack Greer and Preacher McDonald.

Lac La Biche Mission certainly worth a visit

September is the perfect time to travel in Alberta—and this year we did. With the reds, greens and gold of autumn, even Highway 63 to Fort McMurray, noted for being monotonously long, was extremely picturesque.

One of the most enjoyable stops we made on the northbound trip was at Winston Churchill Provincial Park at Lac La Biche. The park which includes a swimming area and campground, is uniquely situated on an island joined to the mainland by two bridges and a rocky causeway.

Here we camped for two nights, and it was quite a thrill knowing we were surrounded by a large body of water.

The island is home to an abundance of wildlife, and listening to song birds and waterfowl—especially a family of loons—was a bonus, as was having an acrobatic squirrel do cartwheels on our trailer steps. A black bear was said to be in the vicinity. So, after dusk, we were on the lookout for dark objects moving around our campfire. Fortunately, we never saw any.

Being interested in history, we spent a day at the historic mission, northwest of the Lac La Biche town site—and what a worthwhile experience that turned out to be.

More than two hundred years ago, David Thompson came west and established a fur trading post on the shore of Lac La Biche in 1798. Later, after a series of posts were built and abandoned, the Hudson's Bay opened a permanent post at Lac La Biche in 1852-53.

That same year a Catholic priest, Father Remas, came to minister to the area's Métis and aboriginal residents and built a tiny log church adjacent to the HBC post. Later in 1855, a frame church was built on the current mission site.

From these humble beginnings a much larger complex took shape. The Oblate Missionaries, the Grey Nuns and Daughters of Jesus fleshed out the mission and it became the centre of religion, education and health care for Northern Alberta.

Eventually a farm, flour mill, saw mill, residential school and warehouses (for shipments to the far north), occupied the mission grounds, and from the varied activities carried on at the old Lac La Biche Mission, hundreds of fascinating stories evolved.

One such story has to do with the Grey Nuns who arrived in 1862. During the Riel Rebellion the nuns feared for the safety of children in their care, so they put their charges in canoes and rowed them to an island in the middle of the lake. Here, the children remained hidden until it was safe for them to return to the mission.

Some of the buildings originally built on this site are thought to be the oldest standing edifices in Alberta. Not surprisingly, the creaks and groans of the old rectory lend themselves to ghost stories, and there have been several reported sightings of a priestly apparition who either stands at a rectory window or sits reading a newspaper.

However, the stories were dispelled by our guide, Emilie Chevigny, who has worked as a programs coordinator at the mission for the past seven years. "I've never seen or felt anything out of the ordinary," Chevigny stated. "For me, the old mission exudes a warm friendly atmosphere...and that's all."

There may not be any spirits lurking about the old buildings, but there is a fascinating collection of hauntingly beautiful ceremonial habits on display at the mission. Once worn by long deceased priests, the vestments were found in closets and drawers in the abandoned rectory when the mission was designated as a Provincial Historic Resource in 1987. Miraculously these ornate robes are in perfect condition and take visitors back in time to the pomp and ceremony of a bygone era.

The Lac La Biche Mission, also known as the Notre Dame Des Victoires Mission, is open for tours and hall rentals during the tourist season from May to September.

More information is listed online at www.laclabichemission.com

Lac La Biche Mission Rectory

Lac La Biche Museum and Church

My dear friend Angie

My friend Angie turned 101 years old last week. Quite a milestone!

After a fifty mile drive to Rocky Mountain House to celebrate her big day, I found her at an afternoon meeting at the Presbyterian Church, quietly adding her many years of expertise to the business of the day. No surprise there, for Angie doesn't believe in sitting on the sidelines, passively watching the world go by without giving assistance

Born in Ryder, North Dakota on October 8, 1907, Angie (Mildred Angeline Charlotte Karlsen), came to the Rocky Mountain House area in 1909 and has made her home here ever since. During this time, Angie has not only seen changes, but been actively involved in shaping the community into what it is today.

“As a child, I stood beside my family’s small log cabin, watching the area’s first railway track being laid across our farm,” says Angie. “The CNR tracks ran across the swamp on the north side of the farm, the CPR tracks on the south.” It was not until the first trains shunted down those same tracks in 1912, that a wilderness settlement became the town of Rocky Mountain House.

Angie recalls her mother, Hattie, working very hard on their farm, both indoors and out: sewing clothing and raising chickens, turkeys and a large vegetable garden to feed the family which consisted of Angie, her parents, Hattie and Levi Lars Karlsen, stepbrother, Clifford, and sister, Viola.

Angie took her schooling at the old Confluence School, a school which once sat on a slope, east of main street in Rocky Mountain House.

“When I started school, fifty-two students, grades one to nine, were taught by one lone teacher,” she remembers.

On leaving school, Angie took a business course in Red Deer before returning to Rocky Mountain House to work at Cony’s Mutual, the town’s small general store. Next, she worked for Mrs. Patti Good in the town’s first telephone office where phone numbers were single digits and all connections were made by hand.

One day a fire broke out across the street from the telephone office and, while running to help, Angie was bitten by a dog. There was no hospital at the time, so a young man named Jack Edgerton took her to get the wound dressed at Mrs. Stewart’s Nursing Home.

This was how Angie met her “knight in shining armor.” She and Jack were married on August 14, 1938, and from that time on, the couple were known as dedicated volunteers in and around town. During the Second

World War, Jack served in the reserve army; while Angie helped organize the MacDonald of Garth Chapter of the IODE, which sent packages to the troops oversees and helped the needy at home.

Twenty-eight years later, Angie was to receive the first life-membership given by this organization.

For forty-six years Jack and Angie owned a dray business, Edgerton's Cartage, which after the purchase of a Model T Ford Truck, was renamed The Lightning Express. In the early years, Jack hauled mail from the railway to the post office and delivered coal and groceries to local homes and businesses. Because there was no such thing as refrigeration, Jack also cut ice from the North Saskatchewan River and then delivered it locally. During the same period of time, Angie cared for son Barry, kept books for the business and worked as the Assistant Secretary in the town office.

Later on, Jack provided janitorial services to the Rocky School Division, which led to my initial meeting with the Edgertons in 1958, when I began teaching. How well I remember seeing a cheerful man whistling up and down school corridors, dwarfed by the oversized trash can he was pushing.

"This is our school janitor, Jack Edgerton," our principal said by way of introduction, then added, "His Worship, the Mayor of Rocky Mountain House."

Presumably, Jack was the only man in Canada to simultaneously be a busy janitor and prominent mayor in an up-and-coming town.

For me, that first impression has been lasting, because both Angie and Jack were always at the heart of their community, serving others. No job was ever too great—or insignificant.

Whatever the need, the Edgertons were there to lend a hand.

With Angie at his side, Jack (who passed away in

2005, age 100), was Mayor of Rocky Mountain House from 1953 to 1963. During his term of office, water, sewer and natural gas were installed in town; streets were paved and the first arena was built. Many business meetings and social functions took place in the Edgertons' spacious living room where Angie served tea from her beautiful fine bone china.

Among other accomplishments, Angie and Jack were founding members of the Rocky Whirlaway Square Dance Club and, as two of the "Group of Seven," they helped erect (by hand) the cairn standing above Whirlpool Point as a memorial to the trailblazers—the men who first drove a car over the mountainous pass, now part of David Thompson highway.

The activities mentioned above are only the tip of a benevolent iceberg. Consequently, Jack and Angie, affectionately called the "Ever-ready Bunnies for their commitment to the town they loved," received the Chamber Of Commerce Award for Community Builders in 1978, and today have a street named after them, Edgerton Drive, at the bottom of main.

My fondest "Angie memory" comes from 2000 to 2004 when she served as treasurer of the Rocky Mountain House/Nordegg History Book Committee. In that capacity, she recorded over $200,000 worth of transactions, gave detailed accounts of expenditures at every meeting, and (keeping in mind, she was in her late 90s), this fantastic lady never made a single error. Talk about bookkeeping! Wow!

Angie enjoys volunteering. She's the perfect hostess. On Wednesday, as I watched her cut her birthday cake, then personally serve a piece to her fellow church members, I pondered over the fifty years I've known her, and similar to hundreds of others, I'm truly honoured to call Angie my friend.

Passchendaele and Canadian honour

Passchendaele—the latest WWI movie came out in theaters just in time for Remembrance Day. And similar to other folks whose ancestors fought in the First World War, I simply had to see it.

In preparation for the big night at the movies, I spent hours online tapping into WWI statistics. As well, I reread the book my father had written, recounting his experiences at Passchendaele, Belgium.

As Canadians, it's taken us almost 90 years to realize how important our country's military contributions were in the First World War. Although over 60,000 of the 600,000 Canadians who fought overseas in 1914-18, died in battle, our young men were a force to be reckoned with.

The German army feared them, for the Canadians were well-trained, competent and remained calm in the heat of battle.

Military participation in the Battle of Passchendaele exemplifies not only the true grit of the Canadian armed forces, but the esteem other nations held for them.

Having taken Passchendaele Ridge in the autumn of 1917, the Australians were exhausted, so it fell to the Canadians to wrestle the town of Passchendaele from German invaders, something other allies had attempted, but failed to do.

In charge of this operation was General Arthur Currie, who organized our five Canadian Divisions in a successful drive, October 25-26. The 3rd and 4th Division (my dad was in the 4th) advanced the first 1,200 meters, at which point the 1st and 2nd Division pushed forward to secure the town. The 5th Division was held in reserve for reinforcements.

Before General Currie began his assault, he set up separate tump-line units for hauling rations and ammunition forward—a dangerous job at best, since men moving supplies could be easily targeted by snipers during daylight hours.

On October 20th, Lieutenant Farmer, a tall, mild mannered man, came to my father's platoon asking for volunteers for a tump-line unit. My dad liked the lieutenant, so volunteered and in due time was issued a three meter long leather strap called a tump-line.

Used extensively in the Canadian northwest, tump-lines were designed with a wide strip in the middle to be placed on the forehead to take some of the weigh off the shoulders.

Rations came in bags by rail or truck to a base. At the base the bags were tied together in twos and slung over the backs of mules. As the mules could not be taken to the front, tump-liners were required to carry rations forward. Six bags was the load for a mule; four bags was the load for each tump-liner.

On Sunday, October 21, men in my father's unit (50th Battalion, Division 4) were loaded in trucks and taken as close to the frontline as possible. Of this my father wrote, "When we arrived in Ypres, the sun was setting, very red in the west due to smoky air over the city. There was nothing but wreckage all around, trucks, ammunition wagons, piles of brick, splintered timbers and shell craters.

"We started walking up a stretch of plank road,

single file, which had been laid down after the original road was destroyed, and on either side of this were dead mules and dead horses.

"As it was getting dark, we were warned not to lose sight of the man ahead. We left the road, followed a duck walk, still going single file. It was soon pitch dark, and there were shell holes everywhere, water-filled and muddy. We had to grope around these with our feet to find unseen holes. Invariably someone would stumble into one with curses. A big bombardment was in progress to the left front. Couldn't tell if it was ours or theirs. Eventually we arrived at a much battered German pill-box, and Lieutenant Farmer told us to dig in the best we could as this would be our billets for a while."

Holes, dug beside this partially destroyed concrete pill-box, would be the quarters for my father's unit during the big push of October 25-26. And what horrific stories came out of that experience!

Shells rained down continuously, exploding in bursts of flame and nauseating smells of death and deadly gasses. When not hauling rations, my father helped carry the wounded to field hospitals and bury fallen friends, such as Pte. Lucas who'd trained with him in Calgary. My father's brother, John, was killed at Vimy Ridge.

Then, on October 26th, father began hauling ammunition forward. This was backbreaking work, carrying heavy boxes around holes filled with water to such a depth, that a man could drown if he fell in. There was always the shock of stumbling over a dying man in the dark or discovering a decaying corpse. And to add to the misery, it rained non-stop.

At the end of the big push, only four remained of the twelve tump-liners in my father's unit, the other eight having been killed or wounded. Yet, the war didn't end at Passchendaele. In fact Passchendaele was retaken by the German army five months later, and in 1918, when the war ended, father then a machine-gunner, marched with his battalion as victors to occupy Germany.

So…what about *Passchendaele*, the movie? The movie has some pluses: beautiful Alberta scenery and realistic battleground props.

Most veterans would take exception to the movie's portrayal of a poorly trained, physically unfit teenager being recruited to the front lines in the Battle of Passchendaele.

The Canadian army had a reputation for recruiting only physically superior young men and training them well before sending them into battle.

Contrary to movie storylines, it took months to be considered fit for front-line confrontations. Even though my father's battalion was recruited Jan. 1, 1917, these men were not sent to the front until Sept. 2, 1917. Prior to this, they had undergone eight months of grueling training, guard duty and, similar to his army companions, my father scored 98 out of 100 points on the rifle range before combat.

It was a savage war. Gunfire caused most of the injuries and deaths, not hand-to-hand combat as seen in the movies.

What the big screen *Passchendaele* does best is focus our attention on a segment of history Canadians (particularly Albertans), need to take pride in.

It's a movie that encourages us to dig a little deeper into our own history and, in the process, discover how admirably we fight when freedom is at stake...lest we forget.

Intriguing history behind Haunted Lake

Haunted Lake!

Such an eerie sounding name begs for attention, yet I'm ashamed to say, I'd never heard of Haunted Lake until I attended the Central Alberta Museum meeting at Alix several weeks ago.

Although the lake was mentioned only once during the meeting, it was enough to twig my interest. After the meeting I drove two kilometres north of Alix, and low and behold I found a pretty little swamp fed lake, beaten into great frothy waves by a northwest wind.

A sign at the entrance of the park explained why

the lake is said to be haunted.

According to an aboriginal legend, many years ago seven young braves were camped overnight on the shore of the lake.

At dawn they saw a massive buck deer which appeared to be trapped in the ice in the middle of the lake. Anxious to catch this easy prey, all seven rushed out onto the ice.

However, the animal had unusual strength, and when it saw the braves approaching, the huge beast reared up, cut a path through the ice with its sharp hooves and swam to shore.

The young men were less fortunate. All seven drowned after falling into the crevice made by the fleeing animal.

Since then, whenever the ice heaves and groans and mist hovers over the lake, legend attributes these hideous sounds and sights to seven ghosts attempting to escape from their icy grave. Now that's enough to tingle your toes!

For the unbeliever there's an equally interesting story about an unusual home built at the lake more than a hundred years ago.

This was no ordinary house, but a mansion of fairy-tale proportions with peaks, turrets and ornate rock-work.

The home belonged to Colonel Ernest Lindsay Marryat, presumably the first white man to settle on the shore of Haunted Lake.

Col. Marryat was a British gentleman of some means who could trace his ancestry back to William the Conqueror (1066). Marryat was also the son of a British parliamentarian so, after a traditional education of British aristocracy, Marryat was recruited to the ranks of the Royal Engineers in India. In 1881, he was appointed manager of the Bengal and North Western Railways, headquartered at the large military base in Rawapindi.

The Colonel was 60 plus, rich, famous and retired when he came to Central Alberta in 1900 to visit his daughter, who was living in the Alix area. On seeing Haunted Lake for the first time, the colonel was so intrigued by the restless waters that he returned to England, gathered up his belongings, and with his wife and youngest children immigrated to Canada.

Arriving in Lacombe in May, 1905 with 21 huge packing crates containing furniture, china, books and family treasures, he immediately set to work designing a home that resembled the ancient French Chateau he'd admired when vacationing in Brittany.

Barbara Villy Cormack, a family friend, reported, "The building of the house was a major undertaking. Rock and gravel was hauled from Tail Creek. Everything else, lumber, leaded casement windows, bricks for the enormous fireplace and chimney all had to be hauled from the station in Lacombe. (When completed), it was a spacious and gracious mansion, though in several respects supremely impractical.

"It was heated by means of open fireplaces in every room, English style, and (in winter) the members of the family were kept well employed hauling coal and ashes.

"There were long roomy halls, and the huge living room had a beamed ceiling with large fireplace at one end. Under the mantle was carved the old Breton motto: "Faith for God...the Hearth for friends."

Imagine the shock other settlers had when they stumbled across this amazing building in the heart of a wilderness. Alberta had only just become a province in 1905, and here was a virtual castle, capped with a pointed tower and multiple turrets. It was little wonder neighbours in log cabins dubbed it, "Marryat's Folly."

Yet time has a way of erasing man-made edifices.

When Colonel Marryat died in 1916, his wife retired to B. C. The land was rented and, as Mrs. McCormick commented sadly, "The house was allowed to run down to a depressing shabbiness," until at last, "its glory faded from the earth."

Although Colonel Marryat is all but forgotten, his daughter, Irene Parlby, gained long-lasting fame as the first woman in Alberta to hold a seat in the Alberta Legislature.

She was also one of the Famous Five who fought in the Supreme Court of Canada and England's Privy Council to raise the status of women by having the word "person" legally include women. This legislation was beneficial to women throughout the world.

Haunted Lake has also stood the test of time. Whether you're interested in stories from the past or outdoor fun, this riparian beauty with its modern campground, picnic facilities and rich history, will remain a great place to visit for years to come.

Christmas a time for fond memories.

Christmas, there's no better time to remember old friends and some of the heart warming stories they used to tell.

Such was the case this past week when I came across a favourite keepsake, a beautiful hand-sewn quilt, a gift from a dear friend who passed away in 2002.

Seeing the quilt reminded me of my friend, Wilma, the many good visits we had and the Christmas story she loved to tell.

The story unfolded in 1940 when Wilma was a new bride living in Trafford, Pennsylvania.

Her husband, George, was an only child who had never really left home, so the young couple shared living quarters with George's widowed mother who still made it her business to direct her son's activities. Not that Wilma seemed to mind the arrangement, as her mother-in-law was generous to a fault.

Some years before, George's uncle contracted tuberculosis. In early times it was commonly believed mountain air improved the chances of recovery, so the uncle purchased a small farm in the Allegheny Mountains. Shortly after, in spite of the bracing mountain air, the uncle died a bachelor and left the property to George, and since George's mother subscribed to various benevolent causes, she invited some ex-cons to stay at the mountain retreat.

"All these downtrodden men need is a second chance, George," his mother explained. "Pay them to cut fence posts, and then you'll be able to recoup your money by selling the posts. With free lodging and honest labour, these misguided souls will become fine, law abiding citizens. Just wait and see!"

Unfortunately, George didn't have long to wait. Two weeks later, when he and Wilma went to inspect the post-cutting operation, the farm was deserted. True to their word, the new tenants had cut a good many fence posts for which they'd been paid in advance. And then they'd gone one step further and sold the posts along with everything else that wasn't spiked down—including the farmhouse doors and windows.

"After that failed venture," Wilma said, "my mother-in-law rented the farm to a family for a dollar a month. These renters were honest, but dirt poor, due to the annual visit of a misguided stork.

"Once, when George and I called on the family, we found chickens running through the house. They chased each other over and under the table, with droppings everywhere. Obviously, these hyped-up fowl, a lone cow and a vegetable garden were the only things standing between ten kids and starvation.

"I remember the wife was so delighted to have company, she gave me a lovely pink bowl filled with butter. I couldn't eat the butter after viewing her kitchen, but I never forgot that poor woman's generosity. To her, the bowl must have been a real treasure because she had so few nice things. Yet, she wanted to give me something and gave me her pretty bowl. It was such a touching gift!

"The following Christmas Eve, this same woman and her husband paid us a visit in town. My mother-in-law was upstairs in bed recovering from gall bladder surgery, so the woman carried her latest infant upstairs to pay the rent.

"Since they had brought a live chicken as a gift, I wondered what I could give them in return. And then what seemed like a good idea came to me. I'd been baking Christmas goodies for weeks, stowing half the baking as well as groceries in the kitchen pantry downstairs and half in a cupboard upstairs. Why not give this poor family half of what we had. After all, the food in the cupboard upstairs would be enough for our own needs.

"With that thought in mind, I loaded the man down with everything from the pantry. Presently, the woman came downstairs, still holding the baby, but dragging a large bag. It was then I realized my mother-in-law had given away every crumb stored in the cupboard upstairs. She'd also added a sizable amount to the rent money before handing it back, but that was neither here nor there. The fact remained, it was Christmas Eve and there wasn't a scrap of food in the house.

"Of course we had a good laugh. What else could we do? After that we always referred to 1940 as the year our Christmas went to the mountains.

"What upset my mother-in-law wasn't the lack of food," Wilma said. "It was the fact she'd been too ill to go shopping that really bothered her.

"She'd sent me out to buy gifts for friends and family, so that had been taken care of, but she hadn't been able to buy a gift for me. I assured her I didn't need a gift. All the same she dug through her trunk that night, and in the morning I found this quilt at the top of the stairs with a note pinned to it wishing me a happy Christmas."

"I have no idea who made the quilt," Wilma continued. "I'm quite certain my mother-in-law didn't. She didn't do needlework; her hobby was reading, but I believe she had the quilt tucked away for many years before she gave it to me. I simply never asked any questions for fear she'd think I didn't appreciate a gift that wasn't brand new."

At that point, Wilma put the quilt in my lap. "My gift to you," she said. "It's not new, but I want you to have it."

Tears filled my eyes as I attempted to thank her. Although the gift was a true gift from the heart and needed no further explanation, I still find myself wondering about the quilt's maker. How long ago, and how may hours did unknown hands toil over this beautiful keepsake?

Did the quilter sing as she worked, and does the quilt reflect the happiness she passed down to others? There's no sign of machine stitching anywhere on the quilt, so presumably the quilter never owned a sewing machine.

Each piece of quilted fabric is no larger than a loonie, yet when joined with tiny, evenly spaced, stitches, they create a work of art that holds as many secrets as Christmas memories.

Quilt pattern: Grandmother's Flower Garden

Musical museum strikes a cord with visitors

Forty odd years ago, when I still had little bounders under foot, summer holidays meant "camping."

Invariably our travels took us into British Columbia where we'd visit such spots as the Enchanted Forest and Three Valley Gap, before picking cherries, peaches, apples and apricots off "weal twees," as the kids used to say.

Those were wonderful times—sunny days of tents, burned marshmallows and toddlers—which seemed to slip away far too quickly.

Remembering those good ol' days, my husband and I decided to "glance in our own rear-view mirror," this past summer and retrace our footsteps into our neighbouring province.

Although traffic has multiplied a hundred fold, some things never change. B.C.'s mountains are every bit as beautiful, the fruit every bit as tasty and, by the number of Wild Rose license plates we saw on the streets, it's safe to say thousands of Albertans continue to vacation in Canada's most westerly province.

We also found the Enchanted forest just as intriguing as ever, with more figurines under larger trees, while a man named Gordon Bell accomplished a phenomenal feat by building an enormous holiday resort at Three Valley Gap.

Except for the help of an industrious wife, Bell, who began constructing his dream by hauling mine cars from Nordegg, 40 years ago, built this beautiful resort without a cent of government money.

At the time of his sudden passing in 2007, Bell was still adding to his museum which includes a village of historic buildings, an immense display center and a roundhouse complete with trains from various eras—even the touring car Trudeau rode in when he gave Western Canada his famous one-finger salute. Very, very interesting and well worth the small admission charge!

Next we spent a most rewarding day at Revelstoke's most recent tourist attraction—a magical, musical museum, otherwise known as the Nickelodeon Museum. The only musical repository of its kind in Canada it's definitely a "must see" for vacationing Albertans.

This museum is deeply-rooted in history, beginning with the building itself which was built at a cost of $28,000 in 1911 when the west was young and customers were definitely on the wild side. Originally, the building housed entertainment for men only: a billiard and pool room on the lower level and, on the main floor, a barber shop, bowling alley and first class tobacco shop. On the very top floor, were seven compartments, plumbed with hot and cold water.

One can well imagine the high jinx this grand old building has seen in the past century, having accommodated gaming, dancing and heaven knows what other activities. Certainly the antique metal ceiling and ancient globe fittings look mysterious enough to make a visitor wonder.

David, Leslie and Michael Evans searched the world over for the perfect repository in which to house their musical artefacts before they discovered this historical building.

Their large collection of instruments required a spacious building with an exceptionally high ceiling to accommodate their tallest chattel—a magnificent 18 foot tall pipe organ, which was specially constructed in 1913 for the Marquis of Camden in Kent, England.

"The building has character, and the beautiful little mountain town has a delightful history," says David. "So, we purchased the building in 2002."

Following this exciting acquisition, the Evans family loaded four ocean-going containers with instruments from their former home in Hampshire, UK, opened the Nickelodeon Museum in Revelstoke and have happily entertained visitors ever since.

Spanning the time frame between 1700 and 1950, the instruments range from the earliest player pianos, such as the Debain which once sat in the opulent home of Napoleon III, right up to the Nickelodeons which heralded a modern pop-culture.

You need to see this collection to believe such delightful instruments still exist. There are hundreds of items: 18th century barrel organs, 20th Century Whirlizers, musical clocks, phonographs, magic lanterns—the list goes on. Many have been restored by Evans, himself.

On your next trip west, plan to visit this latest, one-of-a kind attraction—the Nickelodeon Museum. It's a musical experience you won't want to miss.

David Evans proudly shows visitors the Debain player piano that once belonged to Napoleon the Great.

Lund family experience several tragedies

It was spring 2006, and the last drops of rain were falling as I turned my car off Hwy 11 a few meters west of Alhambra Service Station and started down Range Road 55, where the gravel pooled with water from an earlier, heavier downpour.

I was immediately struck with the lovely landscape, the lush green grass and aspen bordering the fields, smelling fresh and new as countryside does in the spring of the year—especially after a rain.

A mile farther down the road I approached the Little Horseguard Creek, which snakes lazily under a small bridge. Off to the right, I could see an old log house, its roof and western walls sagging, belying its days of hustle and bustle when small children romped on the floor and a busy housewife took pans of freshly baked bread from the oven of a wood-burning cook stove.

This log building, situated on the NE 30-38-W5, was built in 1907 by Helge Lund, and it served as a home for the Lund family for many years after their immigration to Central Alberta from North Dakota in 1906.

Helge Lund was a Norwegian by birth who came with his parents and siblings to America when he was about four years old. As a young man, Helge attended Carlton College in Minnesota and was later employed as an auditor, a deputy clerk and deputy assessor.

After he married Ingeborg Gjefle on April 6, 1893, the young couple moved to North Dakota and farmed in partnership with a brother. Because the venture was unproductive, Helge, his wife and seven children came to Central Alberta with Helge's uncle, Ivar Lund, and Ivar's wife and six children. These two Lund families were the first settlers in the Alhambra-Horseguard district.

Helge and his family lived in a tent when they first arrived, then a shelter which was later used for a barn, before building the one and a half story log home which, today, is making its final stand. Helge bought several cows and four horses, the latter being used for farm work and transportation. Instead of planting trees, as the family had done in North Dakota, they cut down trees with an axe and saw—clearing land—so they could "prove up" on their homestead.

Freighters and other settlers traveling to and from the Rocky Mountain House area had to cross the Horseguard Creek right in front of the Lund's log house, and Ingeborg often served meals to weary travelers who came by in horse drawn conveyances.

Tragedy struck the family on January 16, 1916,

when Helge suddenly became ill and died from an undiagnosed illness. Two years later, in 1918, the Spanish influenza epidemic broke out in Central Alberta, and Lottie, the eldest daughter who was clerking at Macdonnell's store in Hespro at the time, contracted the flu and died—as did two of Lottie's cousins. All three of these young people had grown up together and passed away within a two-week period. Such a shock! Such a tremendous loss for the family!

During this time, Ingeborg worked long and hard trying to meet the needs of her large family.

"She worked far too hard," her son Tom remarked. "She had no resistance to disease and died on November 4, 1921, from pneumonia."

Helge and Ingeborg's children were Hilda born in 1895; twins, Herbert and Lottie born in 1898; Sophie in 1900; Olga in 1902; Alfred in 1904; Marie in 1906; Otto in 1908; twins, Nina and Christine (Tina) in 1911 and Tom on July 3, 1913.

Of these 11 children, only Tom's family remained on the original homestead land.

Tom went to school at Horseguard for Grades 1 through 4. After his mother died, he went to stay with his sisters Olga and Sophie in Calgary and took his Grade 5, 6 and 7 there. He then returned to live with his brother Herbert on the homestead and finished his schooling at the local school. In 1937, he married Lizzie (Elizabeth MacDonald) and three sons and a daughter were born to this union: Tyrone (Ty Lund, our well-loved Alberta MP); Curtis, an Edmonton teacher; Sharlene (Mrs. Orlen Von Hollen) and Marc, the family farmer. After years of good agricultural practices, the family has built the farm up to about 2,000 acres of productive farm land and, in 1980, were recipients of the Farm Family Award.

Marc Lund, grandson of Helge and Ingeborg, farms the original homestead plus many more acres with his wife and three daughters. The girls travel to school in Rocky Mountain House by car, truck or school bus—modern transportation very different from that used by their great-grandparents.

After leaving the Lunds' home, I stopped at the Little Horseguard Cemetery which lies across the road from their farm site. The cemetery is a beautiful spot with neatly trimmed grass and wild flowers shaded by tall aspen trees. Here beneath grey headstones, rest the earthly remains of nine of the original Lund family: Parents, Helge and Ingeborg and seven of their children: Herbert, Lottie, Olga, Alfred, Otto, Christine and Tom, the youngest who passed away in 2008.

From the cemetery one can see the aging log house. More than 90 years ago, Tom was born in this house, and Helge and Ingeborg died in the house. To be sure its roof is sagging, but it is still an intriguing old fortress—a building that signifies a century old commitment to family and community by immigrants, Helge and Ingeborg Lund and their industrious descendants.

Aurora School served the community well

Aurora, it was quite a landmark in its day!

However a new era has dawned, and the laughter of school children no longer echoes from the knoll at the base of the hill, affectionately named Ol' Kinni. No, not the way it used to, but those happy sounds still linger in the minds of former students who learned to read and write in that old log schoolhouse on the hill.

Aurora School, fifteen miles north of Leslieville, was said to have been named by a local resident, Mrs. Sherman, in May of 1917, when a new school district, #3478, was formed to educate the offspring of the area's earliest settlers.

No doubt Mrs. Sherman had great hopes for the

school since “aurora,” means the dawn of something special, a word derived from the ancient Greek goddess of dawn, Aurora. Perhaps this thoughtful pioneer lady even imagined educated children shooting across the hemisphere like northern lights (aurora borealis), brightening dark, illiterate places. No one knows her exact thoughts, but we know the name “Aurora” was adopted before the building of a schoolhouse.

In the beginning, classes were held in two small frame buildings, utilized at different times, and school commenced in 1917 with nine pupils enrolled in three grades: Carna Sherman, Alvera Allworden and Daryle Johnson in Grade 1; Ruie and George Randall and Evart Johnson in Grade 3 and Edith Scott, Vera Johnson and Leila Randall in Grade 7.

Evelyne Lees, a wiry little schoolmarm in long-sleeved, high-neck blouses and dark, floor-length skirts, was Aurora’s first teacher. Recalling those days, Miss Lees said, “Although money was very scarce, my nine pupils were clean and neatly dressed. Dresses, aprons and boys shirts were made from flour sacks, washed, dyed, and so stylishly sewn they gave the wearer a very smart appearance.”

Miss Lees went on to say in cold weather her pupils wore warm mitts, socks and sweaters hand-knitted from sheep’s wool. And, in those hard times, “bagie-butter,” another name for cooked, mashed rutabaga (Swedish turnip), made an economic spread for school children’s sandwiches. Taking a lesson from the past, we can readily see there were, and still are, innovative ways to survive during an economic recession.

Aurora’s first schoolhouse was built on the lowest, most southerly tip of what could be described as a small mountain. Known as Kinnikinnick, this huge hill was named for the medicinal kinnikinnick plant growing abundantly on its sides. It was an unusual location for a school. Situated, as it was, on a steep incline made reaching the schoolhouse difficult even on the driest of days. Yet the log building was visible from east to west, so it could be used as a landmark by drivers of horse-drawn sleds and buggies travelling the Leedale-Leslieville trail.

Teachers who taught in the log schoolhouse (listed by surnames), were Lees, Frith, Simonde, Cameron, Hass, Eritsland, Urquart, Boyer, Chapell, Stollings, Crawford, Simpson, Shantz, Erskine, Cumberland, Serrah, Weekes, Beales, Bennett, Karchutt and Beckett.

Esther Stollings who taught school at Aurora in 1932 recalled some of the small frustration when displaying pupils' art work on the log walls.

"The school had been built of large logs, still round on the inside," she wrote. "And when you thumbtacked a picture (mounted on coloured paper, if you were lucky enough to have coloured paper), you had a choice of putting the picture on the large end of a log and letting the top and bottom stand out in space, or place it on a smaller log and letting the top and bottom curve outward against the logs above and below. I usually chose the first way." Then as if to make amends for petty grumbling, she added, "Actually the school was cozy, and after pink and yellow crepe paper streamers were put up to form window curtains, the school was quite homelike."

As for myself, Aurora's old log schoolhouse held special memories. I well remember my first day of school—Grade one—climbing a set of splintery steps that could be mounted from three sides, then passing unpainted cloak rooms on either side of the entrance until I stood trembling inside the classroom. This was my first glimpse of the infamous log interior, the long flat-topped heater, the shelves of Rogers Golden Syrup pails (children's lunch buckets) and rows of varnished desks on wrought iron legs. A picture of King George hung above the room's only blackboard, and all around came the sound of stomping feet and an overpowering scent of chalk and floor oil.

As I recall there were 38 students enrolled that September with only one small, dark-eyed person, Mrs. Beckett, the good Bible-wielding lady, who taught at Aurora for the next twelve and a half years.

Someone led me to a desk which I shared with two other beginners: Donna Robinson and Katherine Cornforth. Three giggling little girls in one double desk in a log schoolhouse!

For over a quarter of a century, this log building was the community's only educational facility. Volunteer labor built it in 1918 (or thereabout), and the much-used building was nearing its final hurrah when I started school in the fall of '43. Then, in November of that year, a new school with Insul-brick siding was completed in the swale below the log school and we moved down there. Teachers in the new school were Gladys Beckett and Emily Ames.

Still the old log building remained. Perched on the hill like a proud old matriarch, it continued to host dances, church services, Christmas concerts, card parties and bridal showers until it was finally dismantled for scrap in the early 1950s.

Today, due to a host of dedicated volunteers, the newest-old school serves as the Aurora Hall and, true to her name, continues to steer her community towards a bright new dawn.

Danish family faced many challenges

The story of the Christensen family's immigration to Alberta is not the typical rags-to-riches story, but a fascinating tale of a young Danish couple who faced many financial ups and downs in Siberia, Denmark and Central Alberta.

Carl Annaeus Christensen was born in Sindal, Denmark in 1880. As a young man, Carl hired on as a salesman for an international farm machine dealership.

Traveling abroad was every young man's dream, and Carl began by working his way through Europe. Then in 1907 he was transferred to Kainsk (now Kuybyshev), in southwest Siberia, halfway between the larger centers of Omsk and Novosibirsk (the largest city in Siberia).

Surely, the 27-year-old was excited as he crossed the Ural mountains for the first time, likely by train on the Trans-Siberian Railway which followed the old Siberian Route from Europe to China. This route was known as the "Tea Road," owing to the great quantities of tea being transported from China to Europe through Siberia.

When Carl reached Kainsk, he found the area much to his liking, for the town was not only a busy center but located on the banks of the beautiful, north-flowing Om River. The climate was dry with an average daily temperature of 20 C degrees during the summer.

However, Carl would learn that Siberian summers were short and winters longer and much colder.

Later that same year, Carl returned to Denmark to visit his parents, bringing with him glowing reports of his new home in Siberia. When a local girl, the very pretty Nanna Labuhn, mentioned she was looking for work, Carl offered to get her a job in a dairy in Kiansk.

Nanna immediately left for Kainsk and, after working at the dairy for several months, she and Carl were married in 1908.

For the next few years the young Christensens enjoyed the best Siberia had to offer. Carl's farm machinery business prospered, and he hired more employees.

Due to the 1890's construction of the Trans-Siberian railway, Siberia was booming. Merchants flocked to Kainsk with its nearby rail/river junction. Stores and offices were opened, and buildings were elaborately decorated amid the hustle and bustle of modern transportation, communications and entertainment.

Carl and Nanna owned a lovely home. Nanna wore stylish clothes and acquired her very own horse and carriage. She also had servants to help her with domestic duties, and when daughters, Ingeborg (Inga) and Valborg (Val) were born in Kainsk, each of the girls had her own individual nurse maid.

In nearby Omsk, a lavish Siberian Exposition of Agriculture and Industry was opened in 1910 with a complex of buildings and ornamental fountains. Central Siberia appeared to be in the mood to celebrate.

However, the political picture was quite different. The reining emperor, Nicolas II, Czar of Russia was losing popularity; the socialists were gaining power and another political revolt, now known as the 1917 Russian Revolution, was beginning to fester.

The socialists hated foreign investors and called on the Russian people to take back ownership of their

1908—wedding photo Carl and Nanna Christensen.

Pictured immediately below is their store and house in Kiansk, Siberia

Kiansk, Siberia (street scene)

country. Due to this new regime, Carl and Nanna's possessions were seized in 1915, their home burned to the ground, and they were ordered to leave Siberia.

The family left none too soon, because shortly after Czar Nicolas was exiled in the Ural Mountains.

Later in 1918, the Czar, his wife and children were brutally murdered by the new Bolshevik rulers—shot by a firing squad in Yekaterinburg, a town the Christensen family passed through when they fled from Siberia.

Slowly, Carl and Nanna tried to rebuild their life in Denmark, and three more children were born.

Although Carl was able to farm (and his farm home was larger than average), it seemed he and his family would never regain their former standard of living. To add to their worries, prices of livestock continued to fall year-after-year, and Carl felt it was impossible to make a decent living on a Danish farm.

Carl Christensen's home in Denmark

One day he read a brochure inviting immigrants to come to Alberta. The brochure showed healthy crops of wheat blowing in the wind. It appeared Alberta was the land of opportunity.

In 1927, Carl arrived in the Ardley district, southeast of Red Deer. He looked around, assessed the farming potential and, believing he'd found the "land of milk and honey," sent a letter home to Denmark asking his family to join him.

In the meantime he began working for Mr. McTagart who farmed near Content Bridge and, later, he and another Danish immigrant, Magnus (Mac) Hansen, rented a farm from Bob Slack.

The following spring, in 1928, Nanna and their five children—Ingeborg, Valberg, Martha, Carl and Martin, along with Valberg's future husband—arrived to join Carl. No doubt it was a happy reunion, especially when Val married Einer Thomsen as soon as the family were settled in their new home.

That autumn, Carl and Nanna suffered the first of many bitter disappointments. Due to severe drought, they had no crop to harvest—or income. This loss preceded a move to another rented farm owned by a Mr. Kirkeberg in the Trenville area, where the Christensen family milked twenty to twenty-five cows per day (by hand) on a share basis. Once again their hopes rose, only to be dashed by seasons of no rain, no crops and no money. Then came the world-wide financial depression. Many times Carl contemplated returning "home" to Denmark, but there was no money for ocean passage.

Hard times forced the Christensens to move to various other farms near Lousana: Jim Glenn's farm, Mr. Ream's farm; to the Parker house and finally to Eric Stone's farm in the Service School District.

Then, sometime in 1930, Carl met a man by the name of Dan Morkeberg who operated the creamery in Markerville. At Morkeberg's suggestion, Carl and Nanna and family moved to the Markerville area.

They worked hard, and eventually were able to own their own farm, the SE 9-37-2-5 in the Hola district.

Here they built a house and outbuildings, and this farm was 'home' for many years before they retired to the town of Markerville. After their passing: Nanna in May, 1953, and Carl in October, 1953, their ashes were sprinkled in the Rocky Mountains.

Of the children Carl and Nanna brought with them to the new land, all five made permanent homes in Central Alberta.

Martin, the youngest member of the Christensen family was well known in the Spruce View-Markerville area since he worked in Markerville's creamery for many years. Later he married, moved to Innisfail and lived an active life until his death, April 25, 2006.

Although Carl and Nanna Christensen came to Canada at a most inopportune time, they worked hard, prospered and were good, honest citizens. To their credit, their children and grandchildren inherited their work ethics. Although none of their descendants have visited Siberia to date, many have made the journey back to Denmark to visit their ancestral home.

Nanna Christensen beside her home in Markerville

Rocky's 'Wonder Dog' made news

Our last cold snap was such a dilly even my dogs had cabin fever.

However, with a bright new season making its official debut this Saturday, my two rambunctious, four-legged friends and I look forward to enjoying a warm spring stroll.

Speaking of dogs, reminds me of a canine that made history in Rocky Mountain House in the 1930s and '40s. Skipper, a cross between a Russian Wolfhound and German Shepherd was not only a celebrity around town, but the dog's high-stepping escapades appeared in the *Edmonton Journal* under the caption, Skipper the Wonder Dog.

"Skippy (also known as Skipper) is the town dog at Rocky Mountain House," the columnist reported, "and he's no ordinary canine because he takes a wide interest in most municipal functions. A large police dog, Skippy is the friend of everyone in this town of 1,200 people, and all in turn are his friends. He has an honoured place at board of trade and council meetings. At dances his favourite spot is in front of the band's big bass drum."

"Now why in the world would a dog curl up by a noisy drum?" you ask. Well, there's a simple explanation; Skipper belonged to the leader of the band, John Plathan.

Born in Finland, Plathan traveled to Russia as a young man and played with the Russian State Orchestra before immigrating, first to Montana, then to Alberta. During the First World War, Plathan served in the front lines in France and played with the Canadian Armed Forces Regimental Band. After the war, Plathan was employed by Central Creameries in Eckville.

In 1924, he was transferred to Rocky Mountain House to manage that town's newly opened creamery, where he won many awards for butter making.

In 1927, Plathan organized Rocky's well-known brass band and, while in the process of raising a family, he acquired the lovable, gregarious Skipper.

Sylvan Lake's Shirley (Parker) Andreef grew up in Rocky Mountain House and recalls that, "John Plathan's Boys' band was renowned throughout the area. And who could forget the large police dog, Skipper, who like his master, possessed a keen sense of community responsibility. It is said he (Skipper) attended every town meeting. When my mom played the piano in Pickles Yeatman's Band, Skipper accompanied her to all the Saturday night dances. The dog would lie at my mom's feet until 'The Last Dance' was played. Then, like a true gentleman, he'd escort her home."

Apparently, Skipper found his way to public meetings without being escorted, or as various residents remarked, "It's uncanny! The dog is usually waiting on the steps of the town hall on the evenings of meetings and other gatherings. Does he read the bulletin board…or what?"

Wm. Teskey who served two terms as town mayor between 1938-45, answered the question (tongue-in-cheek), by saying "Skipper must be able to read public notices, because meeting dates are not on a regular schedule, and the dog hasn't missed many meetings over a period of several years."

Although John Plathan was Skipper's rightful owner, the dog was a friend of adults and children alike, and it was said no individual could really claim him as their own. "He was a big dog," said one fan, "and similar to most large canines, he was quiet and orderly. Yet, he had a sense of rhythm, and at dances when the music was to his liking he assisted the drummer by thumping the side of the drum with his tail."

Perhaps Skipper made his greatest impression in 1946, during the evening ceremony commemorating the official opening of the David Thompson Bridge. This was a huge event for area residents—a day to pull out all stops and celebrate.

True to form, that evening Skipper decided to take in the grand ceremony and, on entering the hall, spied his pals in the band performing on stage. Long tables ran along each side of the hall, with a head table, decorated to the nines, below the elevated stage. The guests were seated.

Pleased to be among friends, the tawny dog bounded down the hall. Then, taking the shortest route to his buddies, he cleared the head table in one leap, managing to knock over a glass or two in the process. The unexpected performance caused quite a stir until the locals realized it was only Skipper, at which point the perpetrator was quickly forgiven.

During the banquet, the big dog stayed on stage. However, when government officials stepped up to give their speeches, the evening's star rose haughtily, ambled down the line of people sitting on each side of the hall and was rewarded with a bevy of pats and kind words.

John Plathan's son, Alex, says the large greyish-yellow dog lived to be a ripe old age. Even today—over half a century later—many old-timers still remember Skipper, still smile as they speak affectionately about "Skipper the Wonder Dog."

Alex Plathan, Skipper and a friend

'Joanie' a well-loved teacher at Spruce View

During the 1950s and '60s, there was an influx of teachers coming to Alberta from neighboring provinces. So many in fact, an old-timer described the invasion by saying, "Central Alberta's residents were fifty percent home-grown and the rest were Saskatchewan school teachers."

One of the most interesting stories coming out of that decade concerned one such out-of-province teacher. Her name was Joan Hansen, or Joanie as many affectionately called her. However, Joan didn't come from Saskatchewan (which was the norm), but haled from the interior of B.C.

I first met Joan in 1992 when I stopped for morning coffee at Markerville's creamery museum. This pleasant little lady with the huge smile lived a block north of the creamery, and she and her husband, Herb, were two of the regular coffee gang.

Joan enjoyed telling about her father, James Burge, who was born in Bristol, England, and her mother who was born just outside London. As a young bachelor, James worked in the diamond mines in South Africa before being employed in Ghana where he contracted Malaria, a disease which recurred at various times throughout the rest of his life.

On his return to London, James was walking past

a pub one evening when he saw a pretty young lady sitting on a window sill. On an impulse, he threw an arm around her waist and pulled her through the open window. No introduction was necessary. It was love at first sight, and a short time later James Burge and Maude Jones were married. For the next few years the newly weds lived in Africa where their first two children were born. Due to another bout of illness, James was advised to immigrate to either Australia or Canada. He chose Canada.

On arriving with his young family in Vancouver, James worked as a health inspector before deciding to try his hand at farming. Although he'd never worked on a farm before, he moved the family to a hundred and forty acres of extremely hilly land near Gray Creek in the West Kootenays. It was shortly after this move that Joan, the seventh of nine children, was born in the Nelson Hospital on April 10, 1922.

Joan recalled her father's attempts at farming. "He purchased two horses," she said, "Don, a bay workhorse, and Mab, a finer-boned mare which I rode when the horse wasn't working in the fields."

James also bought four Jersey cows and a bull. Joan had reason to remember the bull because it chased her and Maude into the hen house. "Mother and I hid behind nest boxes all afternoon until the men came home and chased the bull away," she confessed.

James also planted rows of young cherry trees, hoping to sell enough cherries and eggs to make a living. However, it was impossible to make a decent income selling eggs and cherries, so he took a job as an Assistant Forest Ranger with British Columbia Forestry.

Joan was fourteen when her father was killed en route to Creston to attend a Forestry course. On this particular day, he was accompanied by his wife and Joan's youngest sister, Ruth. The road to Creston was very narrow and winding, and the three Burges met another vehicle on a sharp bend in the road. James swerved to avoid hitting the oncoming car and plunged over a steep bank. Neither Maude nor Ruth were injured, but James was crushed under the rolling vehicle.

Her father's death brought many changes to Joan's life. The head Forest Ranger (her father's former boss), and his wife invited Joan to live with them. This enabled Joan to take Grades nine to twelve in Creston, while doing chores and baby-sitting in exchange for room and board.

Joan had only just completed high school when World War II broke out. So, in 1943, she joined the Women's Royal Canadian Navy (WRCN), and took telegraphy training in St. Hyacinth, Quebec, where she learned Morse code as a precursor to deciphering German messages. After finishing this course, Joan was sent to Station #1, just outside Ottawa, Ontario and worked as a telegrapher for two years. Then, when the war was over in 1945, she returned to Vancouver before being discharged.

A civilian, once more, Joan went home to Grays Creek to spend time with her family, and after several months at home, her mother suggested she take a teachers' training course. "That's the last thing I wanted to do," Joan admitted, " but mother insisted, so off I went to Normal School—back to Vancouver to become a teacher."

Joan's first job was practice teaching at Crawford Bay, unpaid of course, but nevertheless a memorable experience. This was followed by an even greater event when Joan returned home to Grays Creek for summer vacation and met a handsome young man from Alberta.

Herb Hansen was driving a gravel truck for a construction crew which, at the time, was building a section of highway along Kootenay Lake. Herb had come to the house with some buddies, friends of Joan's brother. Soon Herb and Joan were dating, and on December 6, 1947, they were married. "My eldest brother, Jim, gave me away," Joan said, as she recalled the happy occasion, "and two of my sisters stood up with me."

Herb was anxious to spend Christmas with his parents, so shortly after the wedding the young couple came to Alberta to begin married life in the Happy Hill District, north of Spruce View. For a short time, the newly weds shared Herb's parents' home, until Joan's father-in-law built them a small house of their own. Later, in 1948 and 1949, Joan worked as the camp cook for the Hansens' logging operation at Horberg, west of Rocky Mountain House.

Following that experience, Joan was a stay-at-home mom until both of her children were in school; then she resumed her teaching career. During this time, the family moved to Markerville, to a small house located on the bank of the Medicine River, first renting, then purchasing the house which remained the Hansens' family home for forty-one years.

Joan was a well-loved Spruce View School teacher for seventeen years, while Herb worked at the same school on maintenance. After retirement, the Hansens held 'Happy Hour' for the community in their garage every Friday evening. As well they hosted many rousing coffee session on winter mornings. In 2001 Joan and Herb moved to the Country Lodge in Innisfail and lived there until their passing, Herb on December 18, 2005 and Joan on March 6, 2009.

Friends and neighbors will long remember Joan as the little lady from B.C. with the big smile. She shed rays of cheerfulness on all she encountered and encouraged her students—by example—to become honest, hard-working citizens.

New Canadian family—history in the making

History is being made every day, and nothing says it better than the ceremonies welcoming new citizens into the Canadian family. Such was the case on March 6, 2009, when 107 new Canadians from the Red Deer area (originally from 35 different countries), took their oath of allegiance in Calgary.

Becoming a Canadian citizen was a proud moment for Philip Mora who was one of the 107 receiving citizenship certificates. Philip's new home in Red Deer is half a world away from his birthplace—the land of a million misty mountains, 1000 tribes and superb coffee.

Born and raised in Papua New Guinea, Philip has lived a most interesting and varied life.

His first home, located in Mei Village, near Kerema, Gulf Province, was made of palm fronds and thick cane from the surrounding jungle Although adequate for the tropics, this type of home needed to be replaced every few years.

"Water for domestic use was carried from a nearby waterfall," Philip recalls, "and food was harvested from family gardens or surrounding natural plants, while meat was obtained from animals raised in the village or from hunting. My family lived beside the coast, so fish was also a constant staple in our diet."

Encountering four distinct seasons in a single year in Canada was a new experience for Philip. In Papua New Guinea there are only two seasons: wet and dry. "During the dry season, the weather is insufferable hot, and dehydration is a constant worry," he says. "When the weather turns wet, the malaria mosquitoes surface and plague the population, and roads and bridges are washed out making transportation difficult."

The coastal area of Papua New Guinea is beautiful, yet it is also subject to natural calamities, such as the earthquake-triggered tsunami of 1998 which killed more than 1,500 people and left thousands more injured and homeless.

Other differences Philip notices between Canada and his birthplace are the diversity of people. The first inhabitants of Papua New Guinea were Papuan, Melanesian and Negrito tribes, who spoke (and still speak) over seven hundred languages.

Eighty-five percent of New Guineans rely on agriculture for revenue, with coffee being their largest cash crop. Cocoa, tea, sugar, rubber, sweet potatoes, fruit, vegetables, vanilla, shell fish, poultry and pork are also grown and exported to other countries.

"Growing up in Papua New Guinea was not always pleasant," Philip admits. "For many years Papua New Guinea was a British Colony, much like Australia and Canada. However, at Russia's insistence, Great Britain withdrew from Papua New Guinea, and independence came too quickly." This resulted in political unrest with rioting on the streets—conditions extremely traumatic to growing children.

In 1980, Philip was working for a couple who

were returning to their home New Zealand. Recognizing that Philip would never have the same opportunities in Papua New Guinea as he would in New Zealand, these friends invited him to come to live with them.

Initially he refused to go, then changed his mind and flew in an airplane for the first time in his life. This was quite an experience! After four years in New Zealand, the same friends decided to move to Australia. Philip went along and became an Australian citizen.

Adapting to Australia was a challenge and a blessing. In Australia, affordable food was available at every turn. Philip's first purchase was a huge cluster of fresh grapes, then finding a shady tree, he sat down and ate all of them in one sitting. Philip had never been inside tall buildings, so looking down from upper windows came as a shock, and escalators were definitely scary when he didn't know how they worked.

He also discovered he needed to communicate in English, and it took a great determination on his part to teach himself to read. This he did with the help of the daily newspaper and coworkers who helped refine his pronunciation. Fortunately, Australian sports were familiar, so he was able to join a basketball team and rugby league.

Much later, while vacationing in Central Alberta in 1993, Philip met Darla Layden, a young lady from Innisfail. They were married in 1995 and made their home in Redland Shire, near Brisbane, Queensland, Australia for the next ten years.

"You've not really seen a beach until you've visited the Gold Coast!" Philip says. "There's endless sand and plenty of space for sunbathing, surfing and walking. I'd encourage anyone who gets a chance to visit 'Down Under' to experience the country for themselves. Australia is a very interesting and unique country. Many of Australia's animals are not found anywhere else in the world, and the landscape is as varied as the people who live there."

Darla enjoyed Australia, too, saying, "Koala bears roamed freely outside of our home, and every day they greeted us with a snorting 'pig' sound. They looked so cute on the back fence but could be very vicious. Being a protected species, there was even a 'Koala ambulance service' to rescue Koalas in distress."

With these adventures behind them, Philip and Darla came back to Alberta in 2004. Now, living in Red Deer, they operate Thirst For Paradise Ltd., a retail outlet which specializes in freshly roasted Gorka coffee. Not surprisingly, this gourmet coffee is imported from Papua New Guinea. Besides coffee, the Moras import a variety of handcrafted baskets made from cane grown in the highland region of Papua New Guinea. Woven by men, no two baskets are alike. These strong baskets, which are both decorative and practical, can withstand heat from baking dishes and can be used for serving or carrying items. Pottery is another product Philip and Darla import from the Kainantu region (eastern highlands), with each piece personally signed by the potter. Individual coffee mugs and cream and sugar sets need to be seen to be fully appreciated.

Philip and Darla's shop, Thirst For Paradise, is located at #3, 4621, 63rd St. (back of Riverside Light Industrial). Philip can also be contacted at (403) 358-5256, and will be serving and selling coffee from his concession van during the upcoming Red Deer Public Market. He invites coffee lovers to stop by for a visit and become acquainted not only with his wares, but with the rich culture of Papua New Guinea.

The Mora family's story is yet another example of history in the making. We, who were born and raised in Central Alberta, tip our hat to our latest citizens and wish them well in future endeavours.

How Dead Horse Hill got its name

Have you ever wondered about place names and the story behind them? Take Dead Horse Hill for instance. There has to be an unhappy story in a name like that…and of course there is.

Fragments of horse bones, still visible if one knows where to look, are a grim reminder of 1911 to 1913 when the Canadian Northern Railway pushed westward, and rail grades were built with horse drawn equipment.

Why were such a large number of bones strewn along this hillside? The question is difficult to answer without a smattering of history. In the early 1900s, folks traveling west from "Mountain House," forded the North Saskatchewan River and followed the ancient moccasin trail along the river's north bank. It was a difficult route that wound over steep hills and boggy swamps, but with the river in view, a traveler's chance of getting lost were next to nil.

Then the Nordegg coal fields were discovered, and this attracted railroad companies—two of them. The settlers in the Rocky Mountain House area had long dreamt of having one railroad, but the Canadian Northern and the Alberta Central came west at the same time, staging quite a battle as they spiked their own rail lines down and tore up their opponents. As the editor of the

"Rocky Echo" reported on Feb. 18, 1911, for a growing community, the activity was welcome. "Two railroads mean two payrolls, two gangs to feed, two bridges, two of everything."

The Canadian Northern and the Alberta Central were fierce competitors. Their gangs often worked in view of each other, and rivalry was intense. "In 1911, Canadian Northern steel was far in the lead," said the Echo, "within a mile of Rocky Mountain House, where they found the first barricades (laid by ACR). Three pairs of rails were spiked to ties on a piece of grade, clear across the Canadian Northern location. In front of this breastwork was a barbed wire fence, all belonging to ACR."

To make matters worse Alberta Central had built their own right-of way immediately ahead of Canadian Northern. So what to do? There weren't many options, so in the dark of night the Northern gang tore down ACR's fences and pulled up ACR's rails. And by day, ACR men built up the fences and spiked down rails.

An onlooker described the battle between the railway companies as, "something between a chess game and hopscotch." And the game went on for months, with both railway crews leapfrogging over each other all the way to Horburg, happily destroying each others grades as they forged ahead.

The Echo went on to say, "According to our friends in the Mountview beer parlor, and according to the map on the beer parlor table, the ACR has laid two more barricades on the west side of the river, not far from what is called the chimneys. But the Canadian Northern has the higher grade. The Northern men come to canyons and filled them in, and just as quickly the ACR dig the new grades out."

Just when it seemed the brawl would last forever, a subcontractor went to jail, and a private policeman was employed to patrol the right-of-ways. This amused the Echo's editor who said the newly appointed policeman "had a fine time shooting spruce hens with his six gun and reporting that all raiding parties had been driven off."

Peace at last, but it had been an expensive war for both Alberta Central and Canadian Northern. To cap it off, the real expenses were still ahead. The ACR bridge was to be 2,112 feet long and 120 feet above the water which meant a lot of cement had to be transported from Innisfail, Bowden, Red Deer and Lacombe—all of which had to be hauled by team and wagon because Canadian Northern owned the rail line to Rocky, and not one bag of ACR cement was allowed on Canadian Northern trains.

This left ACR with a huge problem. They had to get cement to the bridge site, so they hired men with teams of horses, mules and oxen to haul the cement at $1.25 per 80 pound sack. Ten sacks was considered a load—and a heavy load, too. "It sure killed off the horses," one old timer said. "If you never saw a dead horse or mule, you never saw those boggy roads to Rocky. Only oxen were certain to run more or less on schedule, and it was a slow schedule at that. The mule skinners left the CNE railroad with 10 sacks of cement and a fresh shave and landed in Rocky with long beards."

Eventually the bridge was built, but in the fall of 1912, Rocky received bad news; a railway commission decided one bridge was enough. The Canadian Northern was allowed to cross ACR's new bridge and go on to the mining town of Nordegg, while Alberta Central (which had recently been taken over by Canadian Pacific) was forced to stop a few miles west of their bridge at a siding called Ullan (known to locals as The Jack Pine), near present day Garth Cemetery.

Now, to get back to the naming of Dead Horse Hill. As previously mentioned, oxen, mules and horses were used almost exclusively in railroad construction, and Canadian Northern employed hundreds of horses each year. Railways could only be built in late spring, summer and early fall. Then as snow fell and the ground became frozen, construction came to a grinding halt, and livestock were held over until the following spring.

One winter—sometime between 1911 and 1913—several hundred head of horses were wintered in corrals approximately ten kilometers west of Horburg. According to an old timer, Canadian Northern hired two men to look after this large herd of horses. However, between poor feed and moonshine making, the horses were grossly neglected. Very few survived the winter. As they died, the horses were dragged from their corrals and dumped over a hill above the original river road to Nordegg. (Hwy 11A and David Thompson Highway had not yet been built.)

When the snow melted the following spring and mounds on the hillside lay bare, westbound travelers were met with a grizzly sight. Shocked by the magnitude of the tragedy, they immediately named the site, Dead Horse Hill. Even with the passing of time—almost one hundred years—the story behind Dead Horse Hill still haunts those who saw the great piles of bones in later years. Sad, but true!

Fifty years of hunting and fishing

I recently came across a riddle which took several minutes to solve. It goes like this. If three men went fishing and hunting from November 7, 1960 to January 5, 2009, how many years did they go hunting and fishing?

My initial calculations were simple: 23 days in 1960 plus 5 days in 2009 equal 28 days. Subtract 1961 from 2009, for a total of 48 years and 28 days. But that's not the correct answer according to three long-time friends who have never missed an annual trip to the west country since 1960. The answer is 50 years, counting 1960 as "year one" and 2009 as the 50th.

The remarkable thing about all this is the fact these three men have hunted and fished together at least once in each of the past fifty years

When their hunting trips began, Charlie Banwell, Bob Vigen and Carl Plehnert were young neighbours, living on farms within a four mile radius of each other, in the Coronation area. No one recalls which of the three came up with the idea, but in the fall of 1960, they packed their camping gear in a one-ton GMC, threw a canvas tarp over the works and lived in the back of the truck for 12 days.

They made their first camp west of Longview, first hunting for elk before moving on to hunt antelope south of Manyberries.

As far as Charlie can remember, the three never discussed how long they would keep these yearly excursions going, but they enjoyed the outdoors and each others' company so much, they just kept scheduling one trip after another, many times hunting and fishing more than once in a given year.

"In 1961 we started hunting moose west of Sundre," Charlie recalls. "And we hunted there for several years with great success. Then, in 1967 we paid an outfitter to pack us up the South Ram River. This particular outfitting business belonged to Irwin Palmer, and Judy Whitford and her sister, who worked for Palmer, escorted us to a campsite named Sick Man's Camp."

Charlie also remembers playing cards one evening in the girls' small trailer at the staging area. When the card game ended, he stood up to leave and bumped his head on the trailer's only lamp—a coal oil lamp with fragile mantles. "Although I caught the lamp before it fell, the mantles broke and the lights went out," Charlie said, shaking his head as his thoughts returned to a pitch black trailer.

"It was a beautiful sunny day when we arrived, but we woke up the next morning to a foot and a half of snow," he continued. "It was hard slogging through the deep snow, but fresh snow made tracking easier, and we came home with a bull elk. The following season we camped in the same spot and came out with an elk and two moose."

In 1969, the three hunters along with several friends, hired 64-year-old Norman Abraham to guide their hunting party along the Big Horn River. Norman was born beside White Rabbit Creek on the Kootenay Plains on August 5, 1905, and his parents and their children were among the first seven original Stoney families to take up permanent residence on the Big Horn Reserve. Norman was the son of the great Silas Abraham for whom Lake Abraham is named.

"In 1969, trees were being burned along the North Saskatchewan River in preparation to build the Big Horn Damn and flood it," recalled Charlie. "And the area was blue with smoke. Norman Abraham was an easy going man and a knowledgeable guide. We had good luck, bringing out trophy elk. Some of the boys went to the headwaters of the Big Horn River and got big horn sheep as well."

In the mid-1970s the three camping buddies acquired commercial licenses to fish at Buck Lake where the commercial fishing season is usually the first week of January. Each year since then, Banwell, Vigen and Plehnert have been casting their nets for whitefish, as their licenses allow, from 8 am the first day until 4 pm the next. In January 2009, the three friends returned to their respective homes with a catch of 64 fish. Banwell and Vigen currently live near Coronation, and Plehnert lives in the Leslieville district.

"We've had many good times in the past fifty years." A hint of nostalgia creeps into Charlie's voice as he looks back over the years.

Fifty years—the same friends with a common interest—that's quite a record, lending credence to an ancient rhyme, "New friends are silver to have and to hold, but old friends are treasures more precious than gold."

Here's to many more years with your friends, Charlie. May the lake abound with fish, the elk continue to bugle, the sun warm your face and the wind be always at your back.

Three good friends on an early hunting and fishing trip in 1961

Still together in 2009

Remembering those ol' Buff Orpingtons

There have been many stories written about livestock (cattle, horses, cats and dogs), and how important these noble beasts were to early settlers. Few make mention of the stoic little creature that bore up so well under the rigors of pioneer life—the lowly chicken.

For pioneer farmers, chickens were essential. They were relatively easy to raise and provided cheap food for growing families. Besides the chickens' practical use, there was also another good reason to have a flock of gregarious birds on your doorstep. Women and children living on remote farms had little opportunity to make friends, but relied heavily on the company of (yes, you guessed it) pet chickens.

When I was a youngster, no farmyard in Alberta was complete without crowing roosters, cackling hens and, in early spring, the cheep-cheeping of baby chicks. Similar to other farmers, my parents raised Buff Orpingtons, an English breed, noted for being prolific layers with lots of mouth-watering meat on their bones. More importantly, this breed was hardy. They could survive cold winters and produce brown, speckled eggs year-round. Buff, black and white Orpington hens had exceptional maternal qualities with each hen raising as many as a dozen offspring in a single season.

Baby chicks were always fun to watch darting

about. A day after hatching, these tiny balls of fluff would leave their nest and scamper after their light-gold or copper coloured Buff Orpington mothers. They had to be fast on their feet to keep pace with the hen. She covered a lot of territory, clucking and scratching, in search of insects to feed so many little mouths. Often a naive chick would get too close to its mother's busy feet and be tossed in the air like a small leaf. At which point, the seemingly repentant mother would stifle the chick's indignant chirp with a worm or beetle.

It was impossible to resist catching and stroking a chick. It had such soft yellow down and tiny feet that tickled your fingers. However, if a chick let out a squawk, the mother hen was quick to come to its rescue with her dagger-like beak and talons. Yes, it certainly paid to be gentle when handling chicks.

If given free range, some hens were masters at hiding their nests—then the search was on. Sister Evelyne and I made a game of it, competing to see who'd be first to find a hideaway's nest, scouting through brush piles and under granaries. Sometimes it was fun; other times it was strictly an exercise in frustration.

Chickens are smarter than they look. I recall waiting for a hen to come out of hiding. Then, when she showed signs of returning to her nest, I followed with the greatest of caution, only to have the shrewd old hen disappear in thin air.

Raising chickens as nature intended was all fine and good, but if a farmer wanted to have eggs to eat during the summer, he couldn't allow all of the hens to raise chicks.

On our farm, we allowed six to eight hens to be broody hens and raise chicks; the rest were laying hens. Hens attempting to nest late in the season were discouraged by placing them in a burlap bag and hanging the bag on a clothesline.

Sometimes we'd have three or four hens hanging from the clothesline at one time. After spending a day in a bag, hens forgot about motherhood and cheerfully went back to laying an egg a day.

Don't ask me why hens abandon their nesting instinct when looking at the world through the warp and woof of a burlap bag. I don't know the answer. I only know this method worked and was widely used.

Speaking of hens in burlap bags, reminds me of a story about a young fellow named Clifford who tried an alternate method of curbing a hen's desire to nest.

Clifford was outdoors, playing with a friend when his mother called out, "Clifford! One of my best laying hens has gone broody. Go fetch her and put her in a bag on the clothesline."

No sooner had the mother gone inside when the friend chirped up, "No use going to all that fuss of baggin' a bird, Cliff. All you gotta do is catch 'er and set 'er tail feathers on fire. That'll scare the dickens out of 'er, an' she'll start layin' eggs like crazy."

To a couple of ten-year-old boys the idea had merit, so they captured the bird, set fire to its tail feathers and turned her loose. Naturally the terrified hen headed for the only place she felt safe—a straw filled hen house.

With more than their share of good luck—and only seconds to spare—the perpetrators of the scheme extinguished the blaze before the straw, hen house and all went up in flames. "We did a real good job of putting the fire out," a much older Clifford said sheepishly. "But I never got up nerve to tell Mom why one of her laying hens looked so bedraggled."

My friend, Murray, tells another 'chicken' story, beginning with, "Did you know chickens can't swim?"

It seems Murray had a grudge against his mother's pet hen. The hen was prone to pecking little boys (probably with good reason), and had given Murray and his cousin some nasty welts, so the two little boys decided to teach the bird a lesson by setting her afloat on Murray's homemade raft on the barnyard pond.

"We only intended to scare the hen," Murray says ruefully. "But, unfortunately, the raft sank!"

That wasn't the only thing that sank. Sometime in the late 1940s, the era of the broody hen plummeted due to the manufacture of incubators. Incubators kept eggs just the right temperature for hatching eggs which enabled farmers to buy chicks by the hundreds.

Orpington hens, which had been such a boon to pioneers, were replaced by chickens devoid of motherly characteristics, such as egg producing Leghorns, and meat producing Barred Rocks and New Hampshires.

In turn, these newer breeds enjoyed a short spurt of popularity on Alberta farms in the 1950s. Then, as years went by, farmers developed a taste for Kentucky Fried Chicken and left chicken rearing to commercial poultry farms.

Unfortunately, all of this agricultural progress has prohibited the majority of today's children from realizing the joy of holding a newly hatched chick in the palm of their hand or raising a loveable pet.

Orvan Thompson returns to his roots

"I used to haul cream from our farm to this creamery in the 1930s when I was a teenager," ninety-year-old Orvan Thompson remarked proudly as he gave his family a tour of Historic Markerville Creamery Museum. Thompson, who was born and raised in the Centerville District, made a special trip back to his roots in May 2009, with his wife, daughter and granddaughter from his home in Madison County, Tennessee.

His parents, Thomas and Mary Thompson, emigrated as children from Denmark to a Danish settlement in Nebraska. They were married in Nebraska and took a homestead on dried-out, hilly land, or as Orvan described the country, "It was so dry bullfrogs never saw enough rainwater in five years to learn how to swim."

When Orvan's parents heard about wet land in Alberta, they sold their farm in Nebraska and, in 1916, moved to the Centerville community, several miles north of Markerville. On arrival, the Thompsons purchased what Orvan refers to as the "home place" where a two-story frame house, a log barn and log chicken house had already been built.

Two years later, in November of 1918, Orvan was born, and this was home for the next nineteen years of his life. Over the years, Orvan's father bought land when it came up for sale and eventually owned 1000 acres.

Two quarters were purchased from the Canadian Pacific Railway. "Good black soil," Orvan recalls, "and some oat crops ran 100 bushels to the acre."

Orvan attended Centerville School and remembers how Delia Fitch, a favorite teacher, made it possible for him to complete his Grade 9 studies.

"At the end of the term, my mother took me to school to collect my eighth grade certificate," said Orvan. "As we were about to leave, Ms. Fitch asked us to wait until the other students were dismissed. She wished to speak to us in private. I immediately thought I was in some kind of trouble. But no, Ms. Fitch felt I had potential, and told Mother that if I returned in the fall, she, Ms. Fitch, would stay an extra half hour each day to teach me Grade 9.

"I was the only Grade 9 student in the community that year and, with Ms. Fitch's assistance, I made good grades in seven subjects in the provincial exams.

"The next three years, I attended Canadian Junior College in Lacombe to gain college entry, but I couldn't afford to go to college. So, after graduation, I went to work at Wildwood, west of Edmonton. One day, I found a 1938 Readers' Digest with an advertisement, saying students could work their way through college in Madison Tennessee."

Once in Madison County, Orvan found the college was, in his own words, "A rundown place, but if a fellow was willing to work hard it was a good place to get an education."

Besides classrooms, the college owned and operated a farm with dairy barns, a broom factory, a peach and apple orchard, a cannery and a food factory where soy products were made.

"I worked my way through college," said Orvan. "And at the end of three years, I was drafted and served as a medic in the army from 1942 to 1946."

Although the Second World War was in progress, Orvan didn't go overseas but served on the home front. "After I was discharged the State of Tennessee gave me a nursing license, and I spent many years home nursing as well as private nursing in Vanderbilt Hospital."

With a ninety-first birthday coming up in November, Orvan can't say he's fully retired, yet. The week before making a quick visit to his old stomping grounds in and around Markerville, Orvan logged 40 hours of nursing at the Vanderbilt Hospital (Yes, forty hours in one week). Not bad for a kid from Alberta!

Keep up the good work, Orvan.

Orvan, his wife, daughter and granddaughter come back to Orvan's birthplace from Tennessee.

Bertha and Allan enjoying one of their many visits to Mexico

Below: Bertha (at right) with Dennis and Annette Gray, and long-time friends, the musical Andersen family.

From Mexico to Markerville

"Hola, Bertha! ¿Cómo está?"

" ¡Bien, gracias! ¿Y usted?" Bertha Thorlakson's voice rings over the phone. It's a pleasure to visit with Bertha in person or on the phone, for she's interested in a wide range of subjects, especially history. In all honesty, Bertha has something of a pioneer spirit herself, considering she came to Central Alberta—alone—at a time when very few Spanish speaking people lived here.

Born October 4, 1938 in Tampico, Mexico, Bertha's ancestry goes back to some of the earliest Spaniards to immigrate to "New Spain." Her mother, Julia, was the daughter of Señor Ismael Davila Cid and Señora Gudelia Molina-Orta. Ismael was a descendent of the Spanish Davila family who came from Valencia, Spain in the 1600s. The Molina family also immigrated to Mexico in the 1600s. They were engineers, traders of European merchandise and influential Mexican politicians. Being well-to-do, they built cathedrals and took an active part in promoting Spanish culture in their new homeland.

Bertha had four brothers and a sister, Julia. As a child, Bertha lived on her grandparents' ranch south of Mexico City and often travelled back and forth to the city by bus. As Bertha explains, "My mother's father raised everything from burros to bulls, all kinds of farm animals including poultry and grain."

She also visited her father's parents who lived northeast of Mexico City on an estate named "Ranchero La Becerra," near Tampico, Mexico. She would travel by bus and ferry over the Panuc River when going to see these grandparents. They were moneyed people and, besides ranching, they owned business holdings and fisheries in Tampico.

Bertha was married very young and, after her baby daughter died at birth, she began a career as the owner-operated of an optic store, selling glasses prescribed by Mexican doctors.

However, she was not altogether happy in Mexico, so when friends offered her a plane ticket to Canada she accepted it. At the time she didn't wish to travel, but kept the ticket. She was glad she did because two years later, when she finally decided to come to Canada, she fell in love with the country—especially the mountains.

Bertha arrived in Vancouver by plane from Mexico City on July 21, 1974. Kurt and Mary Johnson, distant relatives met her plane in Vancouver, so instead of flying to Calgary, she told the Johnsons she would like to travel with them to Calgary by car. "But you will be uncomfortable riding with us," they told her. "You'll have to ride with our three children and sleep in a tent trailer."

"What is a tent trailer?" Bertha asked, and when she was told, she said she didn't mind sleeping in a tent trailer or being crowded in the back seat. "As long as I get to see the mountains, I'll be happy," she replied.

After Bertha arrived in Calgary on July 23, she stayed with the Johnson family three days. After that she was invited to go to British Columbia. Here she renewed acquaintances with friends she had met previously in Mexico. Three months and three weeks later, she married one of these friends, an amiable Dane named Borge

Pedersen.

Bertha and Borge had a lovely home at Shuswap Lake. Together, they enjoyed traveling all over the world. Some of the countries they visited were Norway, Denmark, Sweden, Germany, Tokyo, Hong Kong, Philippians and twice they visited Hawaii. They also toured the States: Salt Lake City, San Diego, Los Angeles, Disney Land and Las Vegas, and one year made a special trip to Pasadena to watch the Rose Bowl Parade. Sadly, Borge contracted lung cancer and passed away in 1979.

Although Bertha had enough money to live quite comfortably without working, she wasn't one to sit idle. While her husband was alive, she had taken up hairdressing as a hobby and completed courses at the American House of Beauty. In the years following Borge's death, Bertha worked in Calgary where she owned and operated her own beauty parlor on Kensington Road and worked in Woolco on McLeod Trail. She also owned a half-section of land near Spirit River in the Peace River Country. This was rolling land, consisting mostly of pasture and hay fields. Intending to rent the land, Bertha struck a deal with some devious people who never paid her a cent. In fact, when she went to collect the rent each year (during the week of the Calgary Stampede which was her vacation time), the so-called-renters would go into hiding to avoid paying her. Knowing these people utilized both the hay and pasture was very annoying, so Bertha sold the land.

Bertha owned an acreage near Okotoks, where she became friends with a neighbor, Mary Munroe. Mary and her husband had a friend named Allan Thorlakson, and it was the Munroes who introduced Bertha to Allan. For Christmas 1989, Allan presented Bertha with a diamond engagement ring. In fact he also bought a matching wedding ring, too. However, when Bertha and Allan were married on April 29, 1990 in Calgary, Allan asked

Bertha to wear a family heirloom during the ceremony—the gold ring which had once belonged to Allan's grandfather, Gudmundur Thorlakson who came from Iceland (by way of North Dakota) to the Markerville area in June 1888.

Friends, Orivel and Svea Rowland (now deceased) were the couple's attendants at the wedding.

Bertha and Allan now resides on the 118 year-old family farm in the Hola-Markerville area. Shortly after she arrived in the district, Bertha joined the Markerville Good Neighbors Club and hosted many meetings in her home until the club disbanded. At present she takes an active part in Spruce View Seniors' events and supports the Stephan G. Stephansson Society. She's a member of Vonin, a women's club; Tindastoll Cemetery Committee and Hola Community Society which looks after historic Hola School. She also enjoys gardening, playing cards, reading and visiting friends and neighbors.

Bertha and Allan have done a lot of traveling in Canada and USA as well as flying to many other countries, such as Australia, New Zealand, Cuba and Fiji, where they celebrated Allan's sixty-fifth birthday. Allan also took Bertha to his grandfather's home in Iceland and enjoyed two weeks of shopping and sight-seeing in that delightful country.

A highlight of their travels was going "coast to coast" in Canada, first flying from Calgary to Vancouver, then traveling first-class by train to the Maritimes. While in Halifax, they celebrated Bertha's birthday in one of Halifax's finest dining rooms. They also make regular excursions to Mexico to visit friends and relatives and often entertain Mexican guests in their home in Central Alberta. So, although Bertha calls Markerville, "home," she still retains close connections to the country of her birth. "I made up my mind to like this country when I first came," Bertha says. "Now, I love Canada!"

A Lancashire lass

Five foot two, copper-brown hair and hazel eyes, this feisty little lady was not subdued by hardship. Born in Melling, Lancashire, England, December 7, 1905, Gertrude (Gertie) Lees's early life was plagued by war and death. When she was eight, her brother died of pneumonia, making her the eldest of the six remaining children. Ten year-old Walter had been her idol and his death was followed by the trauma of the first great war.

From the earliest organized air raids in 1915 to the huge German offensive in 1918, Britain was constantly under attack from the air. Bombs, aimed at the munitions works in nearby Manchester, often exploded in the Southport area where Gertie and her family lived. At the sound of sirens, lights were doused and Gertie and her siblings were hustled to the safest place in the house, under the large, oak dining room table.

Wreckage from ships regularly washed up on Southport's beach and, because adults could be jailed for salvaging, little Gertie was sent to the beach to pick up canned goods which washed ashore. With her father, a gunner-instructor, stationed away from home and food rationed, Gertie knew salvaging was important for survival. She quickly learned how to select the best cans of food. If a can was bloated with sea water, she left it.

She then chose as many undamaged cans as her

small arms could carry—before the beach patrols caught her—and run home with the booty.

Gertie and her mother also worked in farmers fields picking potatoes during those lean years. Later, when Canadian soldiers were billeted in Gertie's home, the soldiers often doled out food from their rations.

At nineteen Gertie married a handsome mechanic, only to be left a widow the following year when he died of peritonitis. Pregnant at the time of his death, Gertie's first daughter was stillborn. Then her best friend, a girl she'd known from childhood, died of tuberculosis.

At twenty-four, she married a Canadian, William Lees, and came to live in Calgary. In 1931, their first daughter, Dorothy, died ten days after birth, and soon the depression struck. Her husband had been a top salesman for Sun Life, but no one bought insurance during a depression, so William went on relief work.

"William was a proud man, and it broke my heart to see him digging ditches and eating in soup-kitchens," Gertie said. So, she suggested they move to William's homestead quarter, north of Leslieville.

Living in the backwoods was a rude awaking for a city girl. The home she moved into was a two-room shack with a lean-to kitchen. When she arrived, a pile of grain lay on the bedroom floor as the building had been used as a granary. Former tenants had cut a hole in the kitchen floor to let water from a leaky roof escape.

Yet, Gertie never complained, but set cheerfully about, turning the neglected building into a home. She made curtains from cotton skirts for each window, then more curtains for the apple box cupboards in her kitchen.

In this house, she raised three daughters, two of which she brought into the world assisted only by a helpful neighbor lady with no medical training.

There was no money for medical care and often not enough to buy stamps for letters written to her parents overseas. In those early years, Gertie dreamt of going 'home' to England, but that never happened. There was never enough money for the fare.

Gertie loved to dance and had a beautiful singing voice. She hosted many house parties, helped campaign for Social Credit and walked miles to attend the monthly meeting of Aurora Ladies' Sewing Circle, the ladies' club she helped organize. When her children attended school, she took an active part in school events. Before every school Christmas concerts, she sewed costumes by the light of a coal oil lamp, for both her own and the neighbors' children. She was a great seamstress, designing her own patterns and making her daughters new dresses from hand-me-downs received from England

Being asthmatic, Gertie was unable to help with outdoor chores, but learned to bake wonderful bread, cakes and cookies in the finicky oven of an ancient wood stove. During depression years, she picked many pails of blueberries, selling them for three cents a pound in order to purchase the binder twine needed to harvest the crop.

As the years flew by, the family's standard of living improved. Her husband became the postmaster and mail courier of Carlos, a small country post office which shared a room in their home for twenty-nine years.

These were happy years; Gertie enjoyed sorting mail and inviting mail patrons in for tea.

Small as she was in stature, on occasion Gertie could present a formidable force. She had strong values and never wavered from them. Insisting her daughters receive a good education, she single-handedly petitioned the School Division for a school bus to transport students to Leslieville High School—and got it.

When her husband became ill with Parkinson's Disease, she was determined to get the best care possible for him. To be close to a doctor, she moved with him to Rocky Mountain House, living there for a year, before retiring to Red Deer, where she continued to be active in community events until her death in 1993.

While in Red Deer, she joined a choir, a book club and, with Mrs. Ethel Taylor (for whom Taylor Drive is named), organized the Red Deer Chapter of Pensioners Concerned, a society which continues its advocacy for improved conditions for seniors. Gertrude was president of this chapter and, in 1976, received a citation and life membership from the Canadian Pensioners Concerned Association.

Although she held a variety of positions in her community, to my sisters and me this little Lancashire lass (as she called herself) was first and foremost a loving mother.

In later life, Gertie and William enjoyed travelling

A special friend with a 'doggone good story'

Denise (Dumont) Bignold may never have come to Alberta had it not been for a barking dog, which only goes to prove everyday occurrences—no matter how trivial—can have surprising results. Such was the case when Denise raced along the sidewalk to catch her landlady's pesky pup and, quite unexpectedly, met a handsome young seismograph worker who won her heart and brought her 'home' to Central Alberta.

Denise was born May 14, 1938 in a small house about a mile from Dumus, Saskatchewan. She says she was delivered by the family doctor who came right to her parents' home for the important event.

Shortly after Denise's birth, she moved with her parents to her maternal grandmother's home which was about eight miles from Dumus and two miles south of Kennedy.

No doubt Grandma Carignan was overjoyed to have the young Dumont family share her home, because

Grandfather Isaie Carignan had recently passed away, and Grandma was confined to a wheelchair.

About four years later, Denise's parents purchased a half section of land (six miles southeast of Kennedy and about six miles north of Kenosee Lake). This would be the Dumont's home from 1945 until the early 1970s. On this land, they raised pigs, cows, horses, turkeys, chickens and various other farm animals with the exception of ducks. Denise's father didn't like ducks.

Horses were used for farm work. They were also the family's only means of transportation until motor vehicles became affordable. Initially, there was no electricity or indoor plumbing in the farm home—and no phones either.

"The phone was something my mother missed," Denise recalled. "There had always been a phone in my mother's home when she was a child, so she really missed talking to family and friends on the phone.

"But we did own a kerosene refrigerator, and this was a real luxury. Not all farm families could afford a fridge in the 40s and 50s. So, in that respect, we were fortunate."

Denise was the eldest of eight children born to Wilfrid (1907-1977) and Yvonne (Carignan) Dumont (1917-2006). Their children were Denise (1938), Alice (1939), Yvette (1942), Arthur (1945), Eugene (1948), Eric (1951), Edgar (1953) and Clemence (1958).

Denise's father was born in Dumus, Saskatchewan, as was her mother, who was born two weeks after the Carignan family arrived in Saskatchewan from Quebec. The original French immigrant Carignans were soldiers who fought on the Plains of Abraham, while the Dumonts are descendants of Jacques Gueret dit Dumont (Gueret of the Mountains), a Frenchman who immigrated to Quebec in 1691. Some of the descendants took the name 'Gueret' as their surname, and some took the name

'Dumont.'

The family always spoke French at home. Consequently, Denise never learned English until she started school in Kennedy. Following her first year in Kennedy's public school, Denise and sister Alice went to boarding school for two years at the Catholic Convent in Montmartre. After that, Denise spent the remaining years of elementary school at Highview.

Highview School was located four miles from the Dumont farm, so Denise, Alice and Yvette walked this distance (eight-miles, round trip) until 1951 when her brother, Arthur, was old enough to go to school. Since he was too young to walk eight miles, Denise drove herself and her siblings to school in a horse and cart.

From Grade 9 through Grade 11, Denise boarded in Kipling, Saskatchewan with her dad's sister, before taking Grade 12 at Kennedy High School. After completing teacher's training at Moose Jaw College, she taught in Forget (pronounced Forshee) for a year.

However, Denise was still in Grade 12—a student boarding in Kennedy—when a yappy little dog sparked a romance that lasted over half a century. After their chance meeting, she and Alex Bignold, the Alberta seismograph worker, dated as often as time and miles allowed. Then, on July 2, 1958, the young couple were married in St. Anne's Catholic Church in Kennedy. After purchasing a house trailer in Regina, the newly weds travelled to Calgary where they made their first home.

Yet 'home' never stayed long in one spot. The young Bignolds averaged a move every two months in their first six years of marriage. In this very busy time, their two daughters, Kathy and Patty were born: Kathy on April 5, 1959 and Patty on September 8, 1960.

In October of 1964, Denise, Alex and girls moved again, this time to Fairbanks, Alaska where Alex worked on the Alaskan Slope until June 1965.

Fairbanks saw the last of mobile living for the Bignolds. By 1965, Kathy was ready to go to school, so it was time to settle down. That July the family moved to Sylvan Lake and have made their home at the lake ever since.

Denise was employed as a substitute teacher in Sylvan Lake for six years before working at Michener Center, Red Deer, for twenty-seven years. During this time, Alex operated his own business, Alex's Service & Repair Shop, just off main street in Sylvan Lake for fifteen years.

Denise is a great volunteer and organizer. I first met her through the Girl Guide movement, where she not only accepted leadership roles in the Local and Area Girl Guide Association, but on a day-to-day basis practiced guiding principles by being cheerful, compassionate, industrious and a friend to all.

At present she works as a volunteer with Sylvan Lake Lioness Club and Sylvan Lake and District Archives. As well, with Alex, she is active in various church and community activities.

She is also a great cook, homemaker, wife and mother and says, "I feel truly blessed to have our children and grandchildren living nearby."

Speaking of blessings: Denise's friends, myself included, thank our lucky stars for a certain cantankerous canine—the one responsible for causing a very special person to make her home in Central Alberta.

Author's notes

We have come to the end of the *Rear View Mirror.*

Let's pause a moment to examine the images in 'your' own rear-view mirror and jot down a few of the stories that come to mind.

Ah, yes! There are hundreds of great memories to choose from. Some will make you smile, others will cause you to laugh out loud, and no doubt some will bring a tear to your eye.

The emotions these mental pictures stir up are all part of living an interesting life. And interesting lives are worth recording for those who motor along behind.

If, in glancing in that telltale mirror, you gain a new appreciation for your heritage while developing a compassionate eye for others, then undoubtedly you will be better equipped to enjoy life's journey and steer clear of obstacles on the road ahead.

When our trails cross again—and I truly hope they will—I imagine there'll be a cozy chair, the scent of freshly perked coffee in the air and more stories to enjoy over a cup of Alberta's best.

'Til then, may your highways be filled with love and laughter; may God's hand be firmly planted on your steering wheel.

Annette

Index